P9-CAJ-171

Thirteen Ways to Sink a Sub

Jamie Gilson

SCHOLASTIC INC.
New York Toronto London Auckland
Sydney Mexico City New Delhi Hong Kong

ISBN 978-0-545-32296-6

Text copyright © 1982 by Jamie Gilson
Reprinted in cooperation with Nancy Gallt, Literary Agent
All rights reserved. Published by Scholastic Inc., 557 Broadway, New York, NY 10012,
by arrangement with Marshall Cavendish Corporation, c/o The Chudney Agency.
SCHOLASTIC and associated logos are trademarks and/or registered trademarks of Scholastic Inc.

12 11 10 9 8 7 6 5 4 3   11 12 13 14 15/0

Printed in the U.S.A.   40

First Scholastic printing, December 2010

For my advisors—
they know who they are
and I won't tell.

Contents

Thirteen Ways to Sink a Sub

1

PIT BALL

I slammed the front door, jumped the steps, and tossed my old red kickball across the yard to Nick Rossi, who lives next door. We had twenty-two minutes to get to school.

"I've got the moustache," I told him, clutching its long spidery hairs in my coat pocket. "Did you bring the bow tie?"

"Yeah," he said, dribbling the kickball down the sidewalk, "it's in my backpack. My notes, too. Don't panic. We'll be spectacular."

I'd made the moustache out of fake hair off an old Wolf Man Halloween wig. It was part of my costume for our Social Studies report, which would be a long way from spectacular. But if it wasn't at least good, our teacher, Mr. Star, would torpedo us. He grades hard.

We got to the corner just as the school bus stopped for the

sign. From inside it R.X. Shea yelled at us, waving his arms and pressing his nose pig-flat against the steamy window. Marshall Ezry aimed a paper airplane through his window, which was open just a slit. In Stockton, Illinois, where we live, kids whose houses are more than a mile from school get to ride free. Nick and I live eight blocks from Central School and, instead of paying big bucks to ride, we walk, even on February days that make our ears turn blue.

Nick poked at a pile of frozen snow near the curb, trying to break enough loose so he could whip a snowball at the bus. I picked up my kickball and let it fly at Marshall's window. But we were both too slow. The bus roared off in a cloud of blue-gray fumes, leaving Nick with a handful of ice crumbs, and me with my kickball somewhere across the street.

As we ran to rescue it, the Oldsmobile waiting in line behind the bus honked at us. *Oongk! Oongk!*

We ignored it.

Oongk! Oongk! Oongk!

Nick leaped up like a rocket into space. Actually, he jumped about four feet across a square. A concrete square on the sidewalk. I stepped on it. "Stinkfish!" he yelled. "I caught you! Stinkfish!" The square he'd jumped over was one of those with the concrete maker's name stamped in it. "Laid by Jas. Wiggleton, Stockton, Illinois—1929—," it read. There are lots of squares like that on the way to school and if you step on one, you're automatically a stinkfish.

"I got you. I finally got you," Nick yelped. He picked the

ball out of the bush it was stuck in and dashed down the side-walk, yelling, "Stinkfish, stinkfish!"

I know every one of those squares from my door to the door of Central School because I've walked there from kindergarten through the middle of fourth grade, and I'm very, *very* good at not stepping on them. I wouldn't have got that one, either, if it hadn't been for the stupid horn.

Oongk! Oongk! Oongk! it blasted again, and I turned to snarl.

"Hobie Hanson," a voice shrieked from the car, "you want a ride?" Nick galloped back, yelling, "Hobie is a stinkfish!"

"Nick!" the voice yelled again. "You've got to help us with this humungous box."

Nick and I looked at each other, decided we hadn't heard a thing, and started off full speed toward school, still a good seven blocks away. We had run all of ten squares, though, when the car screeched up beside us.

"Hobie and Nick, you *stop* now!" the voice demanded. We knew who it was, of course. It was Molly Bosco. We were giving our report with her and Lisa Soloman that afternoon. Not because we wanted to. We were *assigned* to be on the same team by Mr. Star, who keeps saying boys and girls should learn to work together. *Aaargh!* Anyway, in fourth grade Social Studies you spend a whole month on Cultures of the World. Our team's culture was China.

"Ho-bie, you left the rest of your rice candy at my house," Molly yelled. She is the world's bossiest kid, with a high squeaky voice that is soprano and then some. It was sticky candy from China, and I'd left it there because it tasted like perfume.

"I'm not supposed to get in cars with people who offer me candy," Nick told her, tossing the ball in the air and bouncing it off his head.

Molly's grandmother, Mrs. Bosco, was driving. Mrs. Bosco is very tall and very fat and deaf enough so she shouts a lot. She had given us the candy to eat while we sat through fifteen boxes of slides she'd taken on her three-week trip to China. Most of them were pretty fuzzy. A lot of them were temples.

Next to her on the front seat was a cardboard box heaped with stuff she wanted us to show for our report, stuff like brass bowls with these flower designs on them, blue-and-white dishes, a cricket cage with no cricket in it, some grasshoppers and praying mantises made out of straw, and a shiny basket that looked like a rooster.

We hadn't moved toward the car, so she leaned toward us and honked the horn again. In the back seat with Molly, Lisa Soloman sat, giggling.

"We always walk," I called, edging off toward school.

"You've got to help us carry this box in. It's your report, too, you know," Molly said, pinching her mouth flat.

"Listen," Nick told her, "we'd really like to, no kidding, but Officer Friendly told us in second grade that we should never accept rides from Mr. or Ms. Stranger Danger."

4

Molly flung her door open and leaped out. "My grandmother," she said, "is not Ms. Stranger Danger."

Nick and I looked at each other and sighed. What else could we do? I shrugged my shoulders and climbed into the back seat. Mrs. Bosco had the front seat pushed as far back as it would go to give her and the precious box plenty of space, but it didn't leave a whole lot of room for the rest of us. So when Molly piled in and then Nick followed with his backpack and my kickball, they pressed me over practically onto Lisa's lap. I didn't mean to squoosh her. I didn't even want to touch her, but when I did she squeaked, threw up her hands like I was giving her boils, and yelled, "Oosick, cootie shot! Give me a cootie shot!"

They're *always* doing that, the girls in my class, when they touch somebody they don't like. I crossed my arms and leaned back against the seat as hard as I could and watched Molly reach in front of me with a tic-tac-toe she made by crossing two fingers from each hand. Lisa stuck her finger in the middle of the criss-cross and Molly squeezed.

Lisa sighed with relief. The cootie shot cured her from getting polluted by somebody as germy as me.

I poked Lisa's arm with my fist to give her as many more cooties as I could, but the cootie shot must have taken effect because she smiled at me. I did not smile back.

Mrs. Bosco started talking loud. She talked all the way to school. "Have you boys had the flu yet?" she asked, not waiting for an answer. "It's on the verge of being an epidemic.

5

While there are always more people sick in February, this is disastrous, disastrous. Why, even in China people were . . ."

Lisa started giggling, and this time I punched her with my elbow. Nick passed me the ball across the girls and I tossed it back.

"Molly, my dumpling," Mrs. Bosco said as we drove up in front of school, "couldn't I just come in now?"

"Molly *Dumpling?*" Nick whispered to me and we both laughed.

"I'm very, very anxious to hear your report," Mrs. Bosco boomed. "Perhaps I could just attend some of your other little classes."

"No, Grandmother," Molly shouted so her grandmother could hear. "Later. *Much.* Come at one-thirty this afternoon. Otherwise you'd have to sit through Language Arts and Science and recess and Music and yucky lunch in the cafeteria. Come at one-thirty. That's when it is."

Nick and I rolled out of the car still laughing at Molly being anybody's dumpling. Then we realized we were early enough to get in a kickball game before the bell rang. That was one good thing about getting a ride, even like that one.

"Thank you for bringing us, Mrs. Bosco," I called in one breath as Molly opened the front car door. I was about to sprint for the playground with Nick when Molly said, "Don't forget the box. It's your report, too."

The dumb box. I slid it across the seat and out of the car. It wasn't all that heavy. Molly grabbed the other side and we carried it easy while Nick hurried up the walk and threw open the door.

Miss Hutter, the principal, was standing in the hall talking to two teachers. She turned and faced us like a wall. Looking over her red-rimmed half glasses, she said, "The bell, children, has not rung, and will not ring for a good twelve minutes."

"But our box," Molly said desperately, letting her side sag like the box was heavy with stacks of bricks and important clay tablets. "It's got valuable things in it for our Social Studies report. *Please* may we at least leave it in the office until the bell rings?"

Miss Hutter looked us over, took a deep, impatient breath, and said, "I suppose two of you may come in with it. But the rest of you must go to the playground."

Lisa hung around the front door. Nick fled, dribbling my ball as he ran. As soon as Molly and I had stashed the box safely in the office, I followed him fast, with Molly and Lisa not far behind.

Nobody else had brought a ball, so the kids must have come flocking when Nick ran out with mine. By the time I rounded the corner, the girl who sits in front of Nick in Mr. Star's class, Michelle, was already pitching one to Marshall with slow, small bumps. He shot it low and past a lot of kids' legs, getting almost to second base before David Trey scooped it up, whirled around, and slammed him out from about three feet away.

I reached the outfield just as Nick came up to kick.

"How do you want it?" Michelle asked him.

"Fast and smooth," he told her.

Michelle threw it just like he'd called it. Nick ran forward and lifted the ball into the air with a really powerful kick.

"Pit ball!" Nick yelled. He raised both arms, clenched his fists, and started to run. The ball arced high over the playground and dropped, *sloosh*, straight into the spit pit, an automatic home run.

Pit balls are the ones that go in the spit pit. The spit pit is this outside stairwell on the back side of the school. It leads down to a metal basement door with a sign that says "Warning: High Voltage Electric Service Station, Public Service Company of Northern Illinois," one of those locked doors you never see anybody go in. It's called the spit pit because kids who wait in line to play, or who have very good aim from practicing, or who just lean over the railing with nothing else to do, spit in it. Sometimes they spit at things. Sometimes they just spit.

Pit balls don't happen often, but when they do there's usually a fight about who has to climb into the gunk. You'd think the guy who kicked it would have to get it, but that's not true. Not only do you get double points for making a pit ball, but somebody else has to bring it up. Supposedly it's the kid who's chasing it, but Molly and Lisa, who had both been following the ball's curve, changed direction as soon as they saw where it was headed.

"Hey, Molly, it's your ball," Nick shouted. He loped into

home plate, smiling like a mad jack-o'-lantern.

"I've got my new boots on," Molly said.

"Besides, it's time for the bell," Lisa told me. "We'll go, like, get the box from the office. You get your ball."

Kids started disappearing like there'd been an attack of killer bees. Nobody else was going for it, so I ran over to look. The pit was, like always, filled with moldy old sack lunches, paper cups, chewed bubble gum, squashed Orange Crush cans, and junk like that. I took a deep breath and started down the .steps, holding onto the railing because it was a risky walk. Even if it was in the spit pit, *I* wasn't about to just leave my ball there. Old gray snow was frozen around the edges of the steps and in the corners, and, in some places, straight down the middle. One slide and you were at the bottom with all the junk.

The bell rang.

"Watch your step," Molly sang as she passed. She laughed and ran inside. Marshall and R.X. leaned over to watch, and I put my free hand on top of my head, just in case.

When I finally reached the bottom step and looked up, everybody was gone but Nick. He leaned all the way over the railing, his arms swinging loose from side to side, and smiled at me, a half-evil, plotting smile.

"Don't you *dare!*" I yelled.

"Dare what?" he asked, grinning wider.

"You know what," I told him, making my way over to the ball, which had landed on somebody's frozen mitten.

"Some kick, huh?" he asked.

"Yeah," I mumbled, squashing a half-dead bologna sandwich with the toe of my shoe, "some kick." I lifted the ball with one finger of each hand, and, without holding onto the railing, stalked back up the slippery steps.

2

SPIES OF
THE PURPLE CAVE

Half my moustache fell off. The right half. It had been tickling the inside of my nose, and when I closed my eyes and sneezed, the right side just flew away like a cyclone had hit it. Off to Oz somewhere. So there I was, hunting around the long table at the front of the class, trying to find half a black moustache. You'd think it would be easy to see on a green tile classroom floor, but it just wasn't anywhere.

I was supposed to be this Chinese guy, Confucius, who was born in 551 B.C. One of the library books had a picture of him in it. His head looked square and, besides the weird curvy moustache, he was wearing a long pointed beard on the tip of his chin. So was I. It was Wolf Man hair, too.

My shiny green kimono was one of those things that Molly's grandmother had brought back from China for herself, and since she must weigh 551 pounds, I could have camped out in it. It had huge red and yellow flowers sewn on it, and Molly said it was too *right* not to use.

We were setting up for the report even though Mr. Star wasn't in the room yet. He was late getting back from lunch, which was weird, because Mr. Star is almost never late. He is big on promptness.

Nick was going to talk about the crops of China for the report and demonstrate how to eat rice with chopsticks. Mrs. Bosco had given him a lesson before the slide show. "Hold the bowl high, sonny," she kept saying. Anyway, he was sitting there eyeing his bowlful of rice when I sneezed the moustache off. After it flew, he sat there chuffing like a laugh box, watching me bird-dog around on my hands and knees.

He was laughing harder than he really needed to. It wasn't all *that* funny. "Confucius looks like Confucius's barber went chop-chop," he said, and slid down on the floor to watch me search.

I licked the sticky space on my right lip, covered it with one hand so nobody could see, and kept hunting with the other. "I don't look any weirder than you do in that dumb bow tie," I told him. He was dressed up like an M.C. for the Ting Tang Show we had planned to do after the report. You have to give a test of some kind, so we decided to put on this TV game show and ask questions about China.

Molly and Lisa were fooling around in front of the table,

setting up the Chinese gong for crashing when kids got the answers right. The rest of the class was shouting, fighting, tossing other kids' books at the wastebasket, doing the kind of stuff you have to do when your teacher, who is never late, is late.

Nobody paid any attention to Nick and me scrounging around on our knees looking for a moustache half. The table we'd been sitting at was covered with a huge purple cloth that was so big it piled up in heaps around the sides. In the front and back it reached almost to the floor. Molly's grandmother had said that the China things would show up *much* better on her purple tablecloth, so there it was.

The moustache wasn't outside the cloth anywhere. Nick and I decided to see if it had slid underneath. We stuck our heads under the table and opened our eyes as wide as we could, but it's hard to find a thin black moustache in a dark tent, which is pretty much what it amounted to. Our bottoms stuck out behind the tablecloth as we felt around in the corners for something hairy.

"You sure it blew this far?" Nick asked. "Confucius sneezes like swift Yellow River." He decided that was funny because there *is* a Yellow River, and his shoulders shook with laughing that doesn't make any noise. He laughed so hard he had to lean back against the leg of the table. I crawled all the way under, too, and the tablecloth flapped down behind me. All of a sudden, it was a violet dark, and Nick's shaky laugh stopped like it had been cut off with a sword. It was mysterious in there. We were hidden from everybody in a deep purple cave, a Chinese guy born in 551 B.C. and a game show host in a red bow tie.

Outside we could hear Molly and Lisa talking.

"You know, I can't believe those guys," Molly was saying, "not wanting to help with the box of stuff this morning. You'd think it wasn't important, like it wasn't practically our six-weeks' grade. Where *are* they?" she demanded. Nick and I smiled quietly. "They were just here."

"They'd better not mess up," Lisa said. "They're always fooling around, like, and I worked really hard on this report until, like, eleven o'clock last night. I used the flashlight I keep between my mattress and headboard and I memorized the names of all the, like, major cities, and major mountains, and major rivers, and I'm going to be, like, scared enough without . . ."

Nick sighed. "She's gonna be, like, a major yawn," he whispered.

"Let's not ever come out," I said, as quiet as I could, twirling my moustache like half a villain. "Let's just stay here in our minor cave and spy."

The class was getting noisier and nosier. Even though the sound was closed off by the cloth, we could have been hiding near a hive of cat-sized bumblebees or under a waterfall of voices. Molly and Lisa were right next to us, though, and we could still hear them perfectly clear.

"They must have gone to the john," Molly said, "while *we* were doing all the work."

"They'd look pretty funny walking down the hall in those clothes. But Hobie's cueshee, though, don't you think?" Lisa asked her. "Like in the car this morning. I think maybe I'll

14

marry him. Maybe when I twist the stem out of my apple at lunch, this time it'll come out at H."

I gagged. Nick made a fist and poked me in the ribs. Lisa and Molly make up these words all the time, and they and the other girls in class use them like they are real words. Cueshee means "cute." Big deal.

"I guess you could say he's cueshee," Molly told her, "if you like rude dwerps, which I don't. I'm going to marry Mr. Star."

Nick and I sat under the table hugging our knees, laughing, watching the girls pace up and down. Then their gym shoes pointed right at us as they started straightening things again on the table. Nick looked at me and I looked at Nick.

"One-two-three-*now!*" he whispered, and we reached under the tablecloth at the same time to untie their shoelaces.

A girl at the back of the class shrieked, "You guys . . . here he comes!"

I could hear somebody setting up a fallen chair and desks scraping against the floor as kids skidded into them from across the room. And suddenly it was dead silent.

3

THE TING TANG SHOW

Under the table it was as quiet as midnight, almost as dark, too. We were both breathing hard, and I was getting plenty sweaty in my green tent inside a purple tent. I knew I was scared because I could hear my heart beating. Mr. Star doesn't exactly string you up by the eyelashes when you do something wrong, but he doesn't pat you on the back and tell you what a great kid you are, either.

For at least two minutes we didn't hear a thing. There was this no-sound that was so quiet it hurt your ears. And then we could make out Mr. Star saying from the back of the room, "Listen, my friends . . ." in that way he has where you know he means the "listen" part, but not the "friends." Everybody was listening. Us, too. ". . . When I am out of this room," he went on slowly, "I expect—"

Then he stopped as the door flew open. It slammed against the back wall, and an enormous voice burst out.

"Is this it? Is this the China room? I hope I'm not too late. Molly said one-thirty. I'm Molly's grandmother and you must be Mr. Star. I can tell. Molly's told me all about your *dear* dimples."

If I could have breathed, I would have howled about the "dear dimples." As it was, I barely managed a squeak. Still, Mrs. Bosco had saved our lives. No way Mr. Star was going to level the whole class in front of somebody's grandmother.

Molly moved her untied shoes away from the long table. "Mr. Star," she called out, "Lisa and I have been ready for ten whole minutes, and the boys have gone someplace." She said "boys" like it was "warts" or "air pollution."

There was another silence, and we knew we had to act.

"Let's break out the front way," Nick said softly, "and pretend that's what we meant to do." I nodded and tried to pull the huge green kimono loose so my feet would be free.

"One, two, three," he began, and we got on our marks like in a race.

"GO!" we yelled together and stumbled out from under the tablecloth like rockets that had misfired.

"It's the Ting *Tang* Show!" Nick shouted as he rose. He flung his arms wide and pointed at me. I blinked at the light, stuck my hands into the cuffs of my kimono, and bowed till my head touched my knees like I thought Confucius would.

The class loved it. I mean, they'd barely missed getting

squashed by Mr. Star and they really felt like cheering. They were laughing and stamping their feet and pointing at me just like Nick did. Even Mr. Star was smiling like he'd just told a joke or something. I smiled, too, like an inscrutable Chinese. And I swear it wasn't till Molly swooped over, grabbed my left moustache by the tip, and yanked it off that I knew what they were really laughing at. At half-moustached me.

"You squird," Lisa said, and I couldn't help remembering that she'd just called me "cueshee." I didn't think they meant the same thing.

Everybody was roaring, especially Mrs. Bosco. She is really very fat, and she looked like a clown giving it the old ho-ho from a squat wooden chair in the back of the room. The February wind outside had blown her black hair around so it stuck out in little bat wings all over her head. And she was wearing a huge raccoon coat that heaped up on the floor like little wild creatures sitting at her feet. Her laughs rolled out, getting louder and louder. She wiped away a tear.

My arms were still in the sleeves of her huge flowered kimono. I lifted them both up to cover the spot where the moustache had been. It hurt. It hurt a lot, like when the doctor pulls off adhesive tape that's been on for a couple of weeks. I took my hands out of the sleeves, locked them behind me, and shouted, "It's not funny!" but that only made them laugh harder.

Molly was steaming. She was even frowning at her grandmother. We were ruining her report.

"Our report on China is about to begin!" she yelled, and, picking up the mallet with both hands, she bonged the gong so loud I bet they heard it in Shanghai. "And the Ting Tang Show isn't until the end," she said with a scowl, hitting the gong again. Rolf, sitting in the third row right in front of her, clamped his hands over his ears. The little blue-and-white rice dishes clattered on the table. "Everybody get out a pencil and a piece of paper because you have to take notes so you can answer questions later." *Bonggggggggggggg*. Mr. Star rubbed his head with his fingertips.

Lisa began. She held up this map of China that was about the size of a piece of construction paper. On the back of it she'd written the names of all the rivers and mountains and stuff. Memorized, ha! She read them off, poking the front of the paper at the same time to point out where things were. Off and on people would stop her and ask how to spell stuff like Szechwan and Yangtze (which she pronounced yang-tizzy), so it went pretty slow. It was, like Nick had said, a yawn.

Nick's crop talk wasn't that much fun, either, for that matter. But he was very good at eating the rice and did like Mrs. Bosco had taught him to, holding the bowl right up there at his chin, shoveling it in with the chopsticks. She gave him a big hand. "That's the way it's done, sonny," she called.

"Oosick," Lisa whispered to Molly.

Then it was my turn. I bowed again, since that's what you do in clothes like that. "I'm supposed to be Confucius," I said, stroking my little pointy beard, all that was left of my

19

makeup. Some of it came off in my hand, and I felt like a shedding Chinese Wolf Man. "Confucius lived in China a long time ago, from 551 B.C., when he was born, to 479 B.C., when he died. They called it the Chou dynasty. He was a teacher like Mr. Star and said lots of famous things that people wrote down. But he didn't say any of the Confucius-says stuff that people are always saying he said.

"I mean, he never said, for instance, 'He who lives in glass house dresses in basement.' They didn't have glass houses in 551 B.C." I waited, but only Nick laughed. My dad had told me that one.

"And Confucius never said, 'House without toilet is un*can*ny.' Write that down," I told the class. "It's going to be on the quiz." Marshall laughed, and Michelle, who sits next to him, did, too, and pretty soon almost everybody started giggling and groaning, but Mr. Star didn't look too happy. He was slouched against the door, and the edges of his mouth were turning absolutely down. I thought, Come off it, Mr. Star, you tell worse jokes than that every day and *we* laugh.

But I decided to quick get serious. It was, as Molly said, practically our six-weeks' grade. "What Confucius really *did* say was something like the Golden Rule. He said, 'Do not do to others what you don't want them to do to you.' Except, of course, he said it in Chinese."

Then I read off a bunch of real Confucius-says things that I'd copied down. I proclaimed them like I thought old Confucius would. "If rulers are good then the people they rule will be good," I said, waving one arm in the air. "Good rulers are more important than laws and punishments," I yelled, waving the other arm.

Now that is something Mr. Star will like, I thought. But he was sitting on the floor so far down I could barely see his face.

After telling about the old-time emperors, I started on my grand finale. "Long ago, the Chinese invented things," I said, "like paper and gunpowder. And they invented this . . ." I reached into my deep kimono pocket to pull out a string of sixteen tiny firecrackers my dad had brought back from a trip to Tennessee. They aren't against the law in Tennessee, firecrackers aren't. They are in Illinois, but he brought them to me anyway to set off on the Fourth of July. "Thunder Bomb," the label said, "made in Kwangtung, China."

I felt around in my pocket for the long stringy fuse so I could fling the whole batch up and it would really knock them out. With my fingertips, I located what I was sure was the fuse, lifted it out of my pocket, and raised it high in the air like a torch. And everybody broke up again. I could have crawled back under the tablecloth. Lisa is right, I thought, I *am* a squird. Probably even a dwerpy squird. Instead of flashing the firecrackers, I was waving my long black right moustache. It must have sneezed itself straight down into the kimono pocket. R.X. leaned forward and poked Trevor's left elbow, and they laughed like I was some genius comic, only I hadn't meant to be funny at all.

21

Tossing the moustache over my head to the purple table-cloth, I reached into the kimono pocket again, and this time I looked in before I pulled out. Fishing out the string of tiny firecrackers, I flipped them to the ceiling, and clapped two times before catching them on the way down. Everybody oohed and wowed. They knew I could have gotten busted just for having them.

But Mrs. Bosco, who'd been sitting pretty quiet in the back of the room, boomed out, "Well, sonny, you better be careful with those. When *I* was in China it was during the Lunar New Year's Celebration and everywhere, everywhere there were dragon parades. The fireworks never stopped. Day and night, day and night they shot them off. And while I have a teeny-tiny hearing problem, those firecrackers were so loud I tossed and turned all night long from the noise. Tossed and turned. Now you may not believe this, but . . ." she said, lowering her voice. And, without thinking about it, everybody leaned toward her to listen, ". . . When I was in Shanghai, just three weeks ago today, I saw a young man not much older than you are, sonny, get half his finger blown off by a string of firecrackers. I was right there when it happened. Right there. The noise was tremendous and that finger flew straight into the air. Straight up. There was blood spurting everywhere."

She leaned back and crossed her arms over the fur coat, looking pleased because all the boys were going, "Gross!" and all the girls were going, "Oosick!"

Mr. Star, who'd been sitting next to Mrs. Bosco, his head against the wall, got up slowly, waved his arm weakly at

Molly, and said, "Look, go right ahead. I—" Then he opened the door and rushed out.

Nick and I looked at each other. Mr. Star had never done anything like *that* before. "Oh, my," Mrs. Bosco wailed, "did I say something wrong?"

You could see Molly was mad Mr. Star had left the room before her part of the report, but there wasn't much she could do about it so she went ahead like he had said. She climbed up on a chair to be teacher-tall and got that I-am-in-charge-here-now look. Then she yelled, to be certain everybody listened. "Everybody, look at me! I've got on different Chinese clothes. My grandmother," she said, pointing to the back of the room, "got these *last* time she was in China. In the year 1980." Mrs. Bosco beamed. "It's what a lot of Chinese people wore back then," Molly went on. "It's called a Mao suit." She twirled around so everybody could see. She had on this blue-gray jacket and pants that looked like too-big pajamas. On her head she wore a cap that looked something like a baseball cap, only the top part was fatter. Pretty nearly every sentence she used started with "my grandmother," and her grandmother kept nodding and smiling and even adding little stories of her own.

Usually when Mr. Star is out of the class we fool around as much as we can. I mean, that's when you can get away with *anything*. This time, though, Molly was standing up on her chair, shouting out a speech, while her grandmother sat on her chair like a fur mountain, staring at the backs of most everybody's heads. Nobody knew for sure what to do.

23

One thing for sure they didn't want to do was take notes. Besides, even though it was only February, the sun was shining. David Trey wandered to the back of the room and got a drink from the sink in the corner next to the windows. He let the faucet run for a minute or two until Molly gave him a dirty look and he sat down. Marshall, whose paper airplanes had won the Fourth of July contest last year for distance, took one from his desk and aimed. It swooped into the air, and then, like it had radar in the tip, glided gently to the table and stuck, point down, in the cricket cage. Aretha Eliott whistled low. It was a great shot.

"In China," Mrs. Bosco boomed from the back of the class, "children are absolutely quiet in school. Absolutely. They are *good*. They *desire* an education." She was like a bullhorn. Nobody said anything. We were quiet. Absolutely. And good. But we didn't much desire an education. Not right then. Not from Molly, anyway.

Molly stepped down from her chair and went on with her talk, holding up everything in sight on the purple tablecloth, all the stuff but the airplane and my moustache, which she flicked onto the floor. When she was finished, Nick took over and said, "It's test time, comrades," and he bonged the gong with a big smack.

"It's time for the TING *(bong)* TANG *(bong)* SHOW *(bong-bong-bong)*!"

Before our ears had stopped ringing, the door opened, but it wasn't Mr. Star like we thought it would be. It was Miss

Hutter. You could tell she hadn't expected to walk into a classroom that sounded like the inside of a bell. Putting her hands on her hips, she lowered her head like a bull about to charge. She did not smile, but peered at each kid like she was trying to decide exactly what was wrong here and whose fault it was. When her eyes reached Mrs. Bosco she nodded briskly and then turned to us and said, "Perhaps you all realize that Mr. Star is . . . indisposed." Her face was grim. "He has gone home for the day."

Mrs. Bosco stood up at once. The fur reached her ankles. I bet it took a hundred raccoons to make a coat that size. She stepped toward the door. "Was it something I said?" she asked loudly.

Miss Hutter was actually flustered. She must have thought Mrs. Bosco had been up in our room shouting at Mr. Star. "Oh, no . . . no. I'm sure not. I'm certain he was already . . ." She looked over her glasses at Mrs. Bosco and said firmly, "He has the flu. Five of our teachers are out with it today and a number of children are sick. Ms. O'Malley, the other fourth grade teacher—in the room next door—is absent today, too."

There are just two fourth grade rooms, and they're across from each other on the second floor at the west end of the school. We're 4B. They're 4A. Another room used to be a fourth grade, but since there aren't enough kids now, it's just used for storage. I had been hearing rumbling all morning from 4A without knowing why, but just then there came a fat *thunk* against the wall followed by a roar of laughter, and I realized that, with Ms. O'Malley gone, those 4A lucks had a substitute teacher.

We heard a second *thunk*. It sounded like those guys were juggling desks and dropping a few. Nick and I looked at each other and started to laugh. That's the thing about subs, most of them don't know the rules the regular teacher's so strict about and most of them don't know who *you* are, so you can really fool around.

Miss Hutter's eyes narrowed. "Excuse me a moment. I have something to attend to." She left the room and almost at once the cackles across the hall stopped like she'd just gone in and pushed the "off" button.

When she came back in she closed the door gently behind her and said, "Class, Mr. Star wasn't sure he felt well enough to come back after lunch, but he did so because he was very eager to hear a report he said you'd been working hard on about . . . pottery, was it?"

"China," Nick said. "The country, not the kind that breaks when you drop it in the sink."

"Oh, yes," Miss Hutter said. "I remember your box of supplies." She smiled at me. "A very pretty kimono." I turned so red I must have looked like a plugged-in Christmas tree.

"We just finished," Lisa told her. "It was very interesting."

"And we are about to have a quiz show, Miss Hutter," Molly went on, "to ask the class questions."

"Oh, that's splendid." Miss Hutter smiled at Mrs. Bosco, and they both sat down on the little wooden chairs and started talking to each other.

26

I got out the prizes. There were five Hot Wheels cars and some plastic models I had made of a Ferrari, an Edsel, and a Model T. Molly set up two life-size cardboard pictures of a washer and a dryer. She'd gotten them from the Maytag dealer in town. They were window displays of last year's models, is how she got them.

"When we call your name, come on up," Lisa said. "You can bring your notes. It's not cheating to bring notes."

Jenny Hanna couldn't remember what Confucius said about not doing to others. R.X. had a hard time naming two major rivers. Aretha knew that rice was a major food, but Trevor guessed that there were 14 billion people in China. When Rolf finally named three Chinese cities, Lisa stepped forward to give him the last car, tripped on her untied laces, and went crashing into her empty desk in the front row. Everybody laughed.

Miss Hutter looked up, but she couldn't tell what we were laughing at. Still, it was like she was typing our names on a computer program in her head called "Troublemakers," so we got quiet quick.

"We're finished," Molly said very sweetly.

"Thaaaaaat's all, folks," Nick yelled, and we all started back to our seats.

"Very nice," Miss Hutter said as she walked to the front of the room and stood behind Mr. Star's desk. "I'll stay with you people until the bell rings," she went on. "You just sit quietly at your desks. I'm sure Mr. Star has given you ample work to do." Nobody moved to get out workbooks or ditto sheets, so she went on. "Tomorrow, Mr. Star will most certainly not be here, so you will have a substitute teacher. I think I know just the young woman to call. She'll be your first substitute of the year, I believe. Mr. Star has an excellent attendance record," she said, looking back at Mrs. Bosco. "A fine teacher."

Mrs. Bosco steadied herself with the bookcase next to her, rose from the little chair, and turned up the collar of her fur coat, ready to go out into the cold. "Today has been inspiring," she told us all, "inspiring."

"Well, class, may I count on you all to behave well with your substitute teacher?" Miss Hutter asked, her eyes wandering toward the room next door, where we could hear a rising hum.

Nobody answered.

"Class," she said sharply, "I didn't hear your reply. May I count on you to cooperate with her fully?"

"Yes, Miss Hutter," we answered all together, like a song. Then we looked at each other and smiled. At last we were going to have a substitute teacher. She could count on us, all right.

4

SVETLANA IVANOVITCH

Burrrgggg! The first bell blared out as Nick and I crossed the street to the school yard. It had been icy cold sliding on the sidewalks, so our coats were hiked up almost high enough to meet our caps. When we swung in the front doors and turned the corner to our lockers, there were Molly, Lisa, and Jenny at theirs, kicking off snow-caked boots and putting on gym shoes.

"Well, if it isn't the Ting Tang Show Peek-a-Boo Two," Molly said when she saw us. Lisa and Jenny giggled.

"Did Mr. Star make it back today?" Nick asked Molly, unzipping his coat. We'd been talking about Mr. Star as we ran, and about what a blast it was going to be if we had a sub so we could fool around all day. Molly raised one eyebrow and smiled like she knew but just wasn't telling.

"Come *on*," I said to her, pounding my feet to knock the numbness out.

Molly looked away and shrugged as though she didn't much care to talk to us, but, since we were being so pesty about it, she would. "Oh, Mr. Star is at home watching the soaps today. Miss Hutter just breezed by and told me what a lovely, sweet young woman we have instead of Mr. Star."

"She said we should be especially nice to the lovely, sweet sub," Lisa giggled, stuffing her boots and gloves into her already crammed locker.

"You know," I said to them, "this may be our only sub of the year. Mr. Star is usually as healthy as a horse. Maybe we should do something special."

"If we're lucky, maybe we'll sink her," Nick said, lifting the knit cap off my head. We all looked at him and grinned. Even Molly. You sink a sub when you make her cry. Almost everybody's been in a class where a sub has cried. You don't start out to do it. It just *happens* when a sub finds out it's the kids who are in control. Grown-ups sometimes can't take that. When they can't, usually they're sunk. You know.

"I think we should sink her," Lisa said. "Hobie's right. It may be our only chance this year."

"My brother," Jenny said seriously, "had a sub once who only lasted half a day."

"OK, we'll go for it," Nick agreed. "If she's good, though, we won't even get a sniffle."

Molly placed her boots neatly on the green paper towels in

30

the bottom of her locker. "I bet we can make her cry before *you*," she announced.

"Who's this *we* and who's this *you?*" I asked.

"The girls," Molly said slowly, like she was working it out as she talked, "the girls against the boys. See who can sink the sub first. Like a video game. What do you think?" She got a brush out of a little flowered box and started working at her hair, which is dark brown and hangs halfway down her back. It had lots of electricity and wouldn't sit flat. Strands of if floated up like there was a magnet in the ceiling.

"What do you want to bet?" Nick asked her.

"I don't know, what do you think?" she said, swishing her hair back and forth like a shampoo ad. "How about M & M's?"

"Big deal," I told her, because it wasn't.

"Money?" Jenny suggested.

"How much?" I asked.

"I don't know. Like a quarter a person?"

"Big deal," I said again. When I was a little kid a quarter was a lot of money, but it didn't seem like much anymore.

Nick, whose eyes had been looking fuzzy, like he was staring inside the closed lockers, said suddenly, "I've got it!" The girls gathered closer to listen. "This is absolutely it." He banged his head with the palm of his hand. "I don't know how I got to be so smart. Listen, we'll bet you this. See what you think, Hobie." Smiling with pure pleasure, he went on. "The losers, who don't sink the sub, have to go down in the spit pit to get the pit balls for the rest of the year!" He stepped back and smiled like he thought his IQ must have just broken 200. "What do you think?"

Molly gulped.

"I won't do it," Jenny said.

"That's, like, gross," Lisa moaned.

"I don't know," Molly told him.

"Why not? Think you can't win?" Nick asked her.

"Sure we can win," Lisa said, but she didn't sound all that sure.

"Look, if you want to back out of it . . ." I started, but Molly couldn't take it.

"No fair dropping the ball down on purpose," she said, and the girls looked at her like they thought she was bananas even thinking about a bet like that.

"Right," I told her. "Only if it's kicked there during a game." I could just see the girls marching out every day and tossing the ball first thing into the spit pit and then leaning back and making the boys fetch it like Irish setters. "Right," I said again. That's what she was imagining, too, I guess, only the other way around.

The girls got in a huddle, whispering, but we could hear Molly tell them how much better they are than we are and like that, and pretty soon they all three turned to us with their heads cocked back, smirking.

"Okay," Molly said. "We'll do it. Too bad for you."

Nick looked at me. "Well?" I could tell he really wanted to.

"Just for today?" I asked.

"For as long as she's here," Jenny said, looking over at Molly to see if that was right.

Molly nodded. "Right. If she's here tomorrow and nobody's won, the game's still on." She slammed her locker door and spun the combination lock.

"If we do this, we've gotta have some rules," Nick told her. He opened up his red notebook and got out a pencil. "One. No torture. You can't bend her arm up behind her back or close the window on her fingers, things like that."

Lisa rolled her eyes. "That's not the way you're supposed to make her cry anyway. That's, like, too gross."

"I think the only rule we need," Molly said, "is that nobody can say anybody else is lying. I mean if I say I'm Jenny so everybody will laugh at the sub when she calls me Jenny and Jenny me, it's not fair to say I'm not, if you know what I mean."

Jenny smiled. She looked pleased that Molly wanted to be called her.

"Or," Lisa said, "if Marshall happens to land a paper jet on the sub's long, pointy nose, none of the girls will tell who shot it."

It was almost time for the last bell and the girls were standing there ready to leave, shifting their feet, waiting for us to answer. Nick and I looked at each other. Then we looked outside. The snow that was falling as we walked to school was coming down faster now. It was a gray, boring Thursday. Why not?

"I guess," I said.

"Sure," Nick told Molly, "if you think you can make the rest of the girls do what they have to when they lose."

"Ha!" Lisa said. "We won't lose."

Molly laughed. "They'll do what I say. Don't worry. And remember, *telling isn't fair,* that's the rule. Pass it on. Anybody who *does* tell gets the silent treatment for the rest of the year—until June. Nobody will say a word to them, not word one. Pass that on, too."

Molly had organized a silent treatment last spring against this kid Marilyn, who Molly said was totally oosick, and Marilyn's mother had gotten mad and called Miss Hutter, and Miss Hutter had had the guidance counselor come to our room. He had talked to the whole class about being nice. We'd had this big class discussion without anybody naming names. Anyway, this year Marilyn is in 4A, probably on purpose. Nobody wants Molly against them.

The three girls turned and rushed down the hall to spread the word.

The last bell rang as Nick and I were hanging our coats in our lockers. So we hurried toward the stairs to the fourth grade hall.

"I'll write a note and pass it around so everybody will know what we're going to do," Nick said as we ran.

"Do you *know* what we're going to do?" I asked him. "Do you think all the guys will do it with us?"

"I don't know. It'll be a blast, though," he said, and I had to laugh because I knew it would.

There was noise coming out of both fourth grade rooms, which wasn't surprising because now both classes had subs. From where we stood theirs sounded much louder than ours. We peeked in 4A to see why. Their sub was talking to this kid at the front of the class. The kid was waving his arms in the air, probably explaining how a panther had dropped on him from a tree on the way to school and he needed to go to the nurse or, if that wasn't possible, the Resource Center. Everybody else was milling around. Their sub was nothing special—middle height, middle hair, middle age, gray dress—plain vanilla.

We looked in our room to size it up. A lot of seats were empty. I wondered if some kids were going to be late. Everybody in 4B was at least sitting down. Molly and Lisa must have been waiting for us. They probably wanted witnesses.

The sub was at the front of the room studying something on the desk. When we came in she looked up. "Hello, boys," she said. "Aren't you late?"

We stared at her from the back of the room. She was about five feet tall and she looked very young. Her hair was thick and black. So were her eyebrows, which practically met in the middle, meaning she was a werewolf. Everybody said that was the sign. She didn't have a long, pointy nose like Lisa said she would. It was a very normal nose, but it was pretty nearly all about her that was normal. She wore a black skirt with colored flowers sewn all around the bottom and a white blouse with puffy sleeves that had the same flowers around the neck. She didn't *look* like a substitute teacher. She looked different. She looked like we should have studied about her in Cultures of the World.

"You're late, boys," she said again. "Nobody else was." She shook her finger at us as if to say, "Naughty, naughty, naughty," and her long silvery earrings shivered.

I did not want to turn around and march back down to the office. I did not want to stand in front of Miss Hutter's desk while she growled. How do I get myself into stuff like this? I thought. "It's not late," I said.

She got a funny look on her face.

"The bells are all messed up," I said, closing the door behind me.

"Besides," Nick told her, standing there looking her almost straight in the eye, "we're crossing guards, and we're always late. We protect kindergartners." He waited a couple of seconds and then said, "We also leave early."

You could hear the class suck in their breath. But we just wandered slowly to our seats, watching her as we walked. She looked at the floor. It had worked. We had gotten away with it. She had flinched. The kids who'd gasped before started to laugh now.

I smiled at Molly as I strolled along the windows and past her desk. "Give up?" I asked. She smiled back and stuck out her foot to trip me. I jumped over it easy, sank down in my chair right in front of her, and grinned. This was going to be fun.

The sub smiled, too. I guess she thought we were being friendly. Sitting on the edge of Mr. Star's desk, she said carefully, "I want to tell you who I am. My name is Svetlana Ivanovitch. Now that is a very, *very* hard name to say, so I had better write it on the board. Then you can all see what it looks like." She was talking slowly in that babytalk voice some grown-ups use with kids, puckering her mouth into a little O. Kitchie-kitchie-goo.

"I was born in Chicago, but my mother and father are from Russia, so they gave me a Russian name. That's why my name sounds more . . . foreign than I really am. Do you know what the word 'foreign' means?"

She hopped off Mr. Star's desk and twirled around, her hands on her hips, doing a funny little skip with her feet. The long earrings had silver bells on the ends that pinged as she turned. "What I am wearing is a costume from *another land.* That's what 'foreign' means. *From another land.* It is a very, very old dress, and I thought you might like to see it."

We were embarrassed to look at her so we looked at each other and shifted around in our seats. She really did think we were babies. She had another think coming. I turned around to look at Nick, three rows back. He was writing like mad. Folding the note carefully, he handed it to Marshall, who read it behind a dictionary he took out of his desk, grinned, and then palmed it to Trevor in the next row up.

The sub half skipped over to the chalkboard and, bracelets bobbing, carefully picked up a piece of the red chalk Mr. Star kept there for writing down names of people who talked too much or burped on purpose or forgot their math homework. For regular stuff he used yellow chalk. She wrote in the middle of the board in big red block letters:

MY NAME IS
SVETLANA
IVANOVITCH
I'M YOUR SUB

We all blinked. It *was* a hard name. You wouldn't want to get it on a spelling test.

"Say it all together now," she said slowly, pointing at each word and moving her mouth a lot like we were lip readers. "Svet-la-na I-van-o-vitch." We mumbled along, barely opening our mouths, and then waited to hear her say, "Again, class. You can do better than that. I know you can." But she didn't. A real teacher would have.

"So what do we call you?" Molly asked, without raising her hand. "Svet-la-na?"

"Oh, my, no," the sub said, shocked. "I don't think that would be right. Surely that's not done, is it?"

"Then it has to be either Miss, Mrs., or Ms.," Lisa said, jumping right in there. "Are you married?"

"No, no, I . . ." She pulled at an earring like she wanted to have something to hold on to.

"Well, are you engaged?" Jenny asked, glancing over at

Molly to be sure she'd asked the right question.

"No." The sub smiled weakly like she knew this wasn't the way classes were supposed to begin.

"Then I think you should be *Miss* Ivan-slow-vitch. That sounds best," Molly declared.

"Ivan-*o*-vitch," she said, "I'm Miss Ivan-*o*-vitch."

We all waited. She ran her fingers through her hair nervously, then, smiling a brand-new smile, sat back up on the desk to start over. "How would you like to hear a secret?" she asked, smoothing out the wrinkles in her "foreign" skirt. We waited quietly, though we knew it couldn't be much of a secret if she was telling it to all of us. "I expect you can't tell," she said, lowering her voice like she was reading us a bedtime story about Peter Rabbit, "but this is my very, *very* first time as a substitute teacher." She beamed.

"You don't mean it," R.X. said, trying to be funny. A few people laughed.

"No, really, I do," she went on. "I just got certified last month." You could see in her eyes that she was worried about the babies here not understanding "certified." "The state cer-ti-fies you to teach," she said quickly to clear things up. "When you have all the college classes you need and they are certain you can do the job, you get a cer-ti-fi-cate that says you can be a sub-sti-tute teacher. I just got mine a month ago and you, my dears, are my very first class." She threw her head back and held her arms out wide like she just wanted to hug us all.

We sat there and stared, thinking it over. Her *dears,* she'd

39

said. I decided it would take us maybe half an hour at the outside and she'd be sunk to the bottom of the sea, right down there with the *Titanic*. She'd drift away and then they'd have to send in a substitute for the substitute. She didn't know *anything*, or she'd never have told us we were her very, *very* first class.

"I *love* children," she went on. "I love you because you are so sweet and good." She leaned down like we were first-grade high and pointed at us when she said "you" and back to herself when she said "me," as if that had to be explained, too. "That's why I've told you the secret. So you will help me out and tell me, like the good little children you are, just what to do and when to do it. Then I will do well, and your principal will ask me to come back. You see, because I'm so new, I'm at the very, very bottom of the substitute teacher pool, but, what with all the flu going around, that's who they're calling now." She paused just long enough to smile a tiny, begging smile. "Will you help me?"

She looked like a little kid, a funny-looking kid dressed up* for Halloween, asking for a triple-dip chocolate ribbon, peanut butter, and daiquiri ice cream cone. What was sad, she didn't even know she wasn't going to get it. Miss Ivanovitch wasn't going to sink to the bottom of the sea, just get stuck at the foot of the pool. I wondered if Nick and Molly felt a little sorry for her, too.

Nick was waving his hand at her like he was trying to shake his fingernails off.

"First off, teacher," he told her when she nodded to him,

"you better take attendance and get the cafeteria and milk count going right away and send the flag people down to raise the flag. Hobie, R.X., Marshall, and me, we're the ones who do all that today. It takes two to raise the flag so it doesn't drag on the ground, one guy for the cafeteria count, and one for attendance. And they want that stuff down at the office five minutes ago."

Marshall and R.X. turned around and eyed Nick like he was bonkers, but when he grinned at them, they laughed back. They're always game, Marshall and R.X. are.

"Why, thank you very much . . ." She checked the seating chart to see who he was.

"Nick," he said, "Nick Rossi, at your service."

Molly looked over at Lisa and gagged like Nick made her sick, but she didn't say anything. Actually, the same person takes the attendance and cafeteria count to the office, and it was the fifth graders' month to put the flag up, not ours. But I guess Molly didn't feel like getting the old silent treatment for the rest of the year, so she didn't tell. Aretha, who sits next to Molly, raised her hand to say Nick was lying, but Molly shook her head and Aretha shrugged and gave it up.

Nobody lied about the cafeteria count because we knew they'd discover that one back in the office. If the cooks boiled twenty-five hot dogs for our class, somebody was sure to notice if only eight of them got paid for.

Roll call, though, was a riot.

Maybe Molly hadn't passed the word yet about not telling, but she had changed names, and when the sub called the roll, all the girls giggled when Molly answered to Lisa's name and Lisa to Molly's. Jenny didn't get to change names with Molly after all, and she didn't look too pleased about that.

"Now, my dears, that isn't the way you're down on the seating chart," Miss Ivanovitch said to them. "Mr. Star's chart says Molly Bosco is supposed to be sitting in the second seat next to the windows and Lisa is in the first row *away* from the windows."

"Oh, Miss Ivan-slow-vitch," Lisa rolled her eyes over the sub's ignorance, "that's an *ancient* seating chart. Mr. Star hasn't used that seating chart since, like the first week of school."

"Well, thank you, Molly," Miss Ivanovitch said, and everybody laughed. "I'll just write your name on the chart in pencil so I can remember." And she did. If Mr. Star saw that, they'd really catch it.

Miss Ivanovitch got lots of names messed up, but we were all waiting for her to get to Rudolph Pfutzenreuter, who sat next to me, right in front of the teacher's desk.

"Is it Rudy?" she asked, not even trying his last name. We knew how to say it easy because we'd known him all our lives. And nobody ever calls him Rudolph, or Rudy either. He's Rolf.

But Nick had sent him up another note while the sub stumbled through Trevor Teneick and Michelle Duguid in the second row.

"I'm called by my last name, Miss Ivanovitch," Rolf said, proving he could handle hers.

42

"Everybody calls you . . . Pfutzenreuter?" she asked.

When we poked each other and laughed, she laughed, too, like a real person, and said, "Then I just won't call on you very much. You've even topped Svetlana Ivanovitch."

After Aretha Eliott, she said, "Raymond Xavier Shea." That really broke everybody up. We haven't called him anything but R.X. since second grade when he moved to Stockton. As she finished roll call we began to realize how many people were absent, a lot more boys than girls. "My," the sub cooed, going back to baby talk, "that old flu bug is really nibbling away at my poor dears. Why, *eight* children are sick," she moaned, like it pained her so. As she wrote out the absence slip she told us, "There are ten girls here and only seven boys." She shook her head sadly, and her ears chimed.

Molly smirked at me.

"It's not fair, you know," I told her. "You've got three more than we do."

She was folding a note she'd been writing to Lisa. "Your subtraction skills are truly amazing," she said lightly, handing me the note, which I almost put in my pocket. Instead, I read it. It told Lisa to start a note going about the bet to the girls in the two rows on her side of the room. Molly, it said, would pass one back down the two on our side. Big deal, I thought. We've already done that. I gave the note to Rolf, and he reached over an empty desk and handed it to Lisa right under Miss Ivanovitch's nose. Lisa didn't even bother to hide it as she read.

43

It was nine-twenty-five by the time Nick and I, R.X., and Marshall stood up to go. Miss Ivanovitch waved both hands at us as we left. "Hurry, now, like *good* boys," she said. She didn't want us to stop and nibble the cabbages in Mr. MacGregor's garden. But we didn't hurry. There was time, plenty of time.

5

I'VE GOT AN ITCH

We slammed the door behind us. Nick jumped up and clicked his heels together. "Wahoo!" he shouted. "How's that for escape?"

"Clever," Marshall told him, "very clever, but what do we do now? Hide in the lockers until lunchtime?"

"We can't all go down to the office," R.X. said. "That would look very suspicious."

"Of *course* not," Nick said, rolling his eyes. He strolled over, opened the door of the empty fourth grade room just down the hall, and bowed us in. Last year they'd used it as a teachers' lounge, so a red-and-blue-striped curtain still hung over the window in the door. The teachers had put the curtain there so kids walking by couldn't see them eating mounds of double-chocolate brownies while they graded those math tests that made us gag.

45

At least, that's what Nick said the reason was, and I believed him. But that curtain made the room a perfect place for us to hide. Most real teachers were busy getting their classes going first thing in the morning. But Miss Hutter could be anywhere, anytime—and usually was.

R.X. took the lunch count and attendance downstairs while Marshall, Nick, and I stayed behind to plan. We closed the door quietly behind us.

"You got any rubber bands?" Nick asked, clutching my sleeve. I shook my head, but started digging around in my pockets to be sure. Marshall shrugged. I knew why Nick needed rubber bands. He was the best shot in our class, and his whole supply had been lifted when Mr. Star had caught him making Aretha's braids bounce from across the room. He'd been zapping her hair with little yellow rubber bands that sometimes missed and stung Aretha's neck, making her yelp. So those were gone and Nick didn't have any in reserve.

There weren't any rubber bands in my pockets. Mom turns the pockets of my jeans inside out before she washes them, and the ones I was wearing were hot out of the dryer when I put them on that morning. Mom has been hysterical about pockets ever since a few months ago when I left one bright red and one red-violet crayon in my pants and they fell out in the dryer. The two crayons tumbled around for the whole hot cycle and melted all over my jeans and shirts and underwear and everything. They were new clothes, too, because fourth grade had just started, and I'd grown a lot since third. Those yucky crayons left big blotches of reddish gunk on half my clothes, just about. So a lot of the time it looked like I'd been in a fight and lost. The color had faded some, but if I was at camp, I sure wouldn't need name tags sewn on my clothes. Anyway, that's how I knew my clean pants didn't have rubber bands or anything else in the pockets.

We all agreed to bring some the next day. That way we could shoot tacos. Not the mushy kind with hamburger and lettuce and cheese and hot sauce that drips all over you when you eat it. Those wouldn't work. This taco is a piece of paper you keep folding over and over until it's shaped like a V. You bite the crease to make sure it stays and fasten the ends with tape. It ends up pretty small, about a half inch wide, and looks a little bit like a real taco. It shoots much better, as anyone can tell you who's ever tried to shoot a real one.

Marshall said he'd help by folding a hundred or so airplanes, the kind that soar up high before they dive, long flyers. He was doing it not so much for the bet against the girls, though, as just because he likes to make planes. He'd rather do that than eat. For sure he'd rather do it than work long division problems or give his report on Australia.

"My brother told me," Marshall said, tearing a sheet of paper off the square pad he kept with him, "that he was in a class once where this kid said he didn't speak English so all the time the sub was there she left him alone. I like that."

"It's pretty good," I told him, "but what if she speaks that language? I mean, she's got on this foreign costume. Maybe she speaks lots of languages. You'd get caught right away if you chose the wrong one."

As we were talking, Marshall was folding. What he was folding was not an airplane, but a gorilla. He also makes spacemen, lobsters, kangaroos, and like that, just by folding paper. It's this thing he learned to do from reading a book about origami, which, he says, is the Japanese art of paper folding. He tried, in a demonstration speech for Language Arts once, to show us how to make a crane, but it didn't take.

"You tell the sub that I can't speak any English," Marshall said. "Then she'll leave me alone and won't suspect when I spend all my time folding. Tell her I can't speak anything but . . ." First he grinned, and then he laughed out loud. ". . . Japanese."

"Japanese!" I groaned. "Listen, Marshall, I don't know, but I think there are very few black Japanese, no kidding. Very, very few. And even fewer black Japanese who go around Stockton, Illinois, wearing orange shirts that say 'My Mom and Dad Went to San Francisco and All I Got Was This Lousy T-Shirt.' We have here a substitute teacher who doesn't know very much and thinks we are mere babies, but about this I think she just might suspect something."

Marshall looked down at his orange shirt. "So?" he shrugged. He made a sharp crease in the paper, folded the gorilla's hand over, and hung it on the edge of an empty shelf. It swung back and forth, but didn't fall. "Tell her you don't know anything about me," he went on, "except that I grew up in Tokyo and just moved last month to the suburbs of Chicago so different from my native land. Tell her I'm lonely for Japan so I sit around folding origami to make me think of home. Tell her teachers make me nervous. Then she'll forget I'm there, and I can produce whole convoys of planes. When she drops by to tell me what a good little foreign boy I am, I'll be working on a crane or something else Oriental and she won't even guess. I promise not to crack."

"Listen, if we were going to have anybody speak only a foreign language, it should be Eugene Kim. He used to live in Korea," I told him.

"Wouldn't work," Marshall said. "One, he can't make airplanes that fly worth anything, so what good would it do? Two, he's home sick today."

Nick grabbed his shoulder. "Listen, Ezry, if you mess up after we tell her all you say is 'here,' since that's what you said when she was taking attendance, you've had it, and I mean that!" Marshall just looked blank and blinked his eyes like he didn't understand a word Nick had said.

I turned to Nick. "OK, so Marshall here folds a hundred Japanese jets. Then what do we do with them? I mean, *exactly* what?"

Nick bit his lip and thought about it a while. Marshall sat cross-legged on the floor and folded another sheet of paper into a plane. When it was finished, Nick picked it up and skimmed it toward the windows. It glided and dipped like a dream. "Yeah," he said, "it's hard to decide whether to shoot them all off at once so the whole room is crammed with flying paper, or just to go at it slow and easy over maybe an hour. I think," he went on as he scooped up the landed plane, "maybe we should throw slow at first so she can't tell where they're coming from and then bombard the air so fast she won't know what to do. That should drive her batty."

"Yeah," I agreed, "and batty is close to sunk. It sure is better than the girls' dumb plan. I mean, what's so sub-sinking about changing names? That's nothing. I bet they won't have any good ideas at all. They're practically crawling into the spit pit already."

Bap-bap-bap! There was a loud knock at the door. *Bap-bap-bap,* the sharp knock of somebody who means business. We looked around the almost empty room and saw at once the only place to hide. Skidding across the waxed floor, we opened the closet next to the sink, packed ourselves in, and closed the door behind as fast and quiet as we could.

But the knock came again. *Bap-bap-bap!* We heard the door of the classroom fly open and feet hurry in, sounding like they knew where they were going and why. It almost had to be Miss Hutter. She would open the closet door and see us huddled there and then—I couldn't even imagine what would happen next. She was headed straight toward us. We pressed ourselves against the walls of the closet. Closing my eyes, I tried not to breathe. Next to my ear there came a rap on the closet door.

"Hobart Hanson!" a strange voice boomed. And then nothing. "Nicholas Rossi!" the voice said next. We couldn't tell who it was, but it didn't *sound* like Miss Hutter. Maybe Miss Ivanovitch. "Marshall Ezry!" it said at last, as the handle turned and the door flew open.

"Gotcha, dipsticks," R.X. cackled, sounding like himself this time. He shot his arms out straight at us as if he was starring in *Frankenstein Meets the Closetmen*.

We felt more like The Three Stooges, scrunched up in the corners of that musty old closet that used to hold teachers' coats and wet boots and drippy umbrellas. R.X. didn't need to make us feel dumb like that.

We chased him around the room, getting closer to the windows than hide-outs should. We could have gotten him down on the floor and tickled the sweatsocks off him, too, if we'd had the time.

"Listen, you guys, I heard about something 4A did to their sub yesterday," R.X. said, waving us away so we wouldn't tackle him. And he whispered it to us as we opened the door and looked both ways to see if anyone was coming.

"No kidding, though, you think we're gonna pull this off?" I asked Nick as we reached the room. "Only seven boys and one of them doesn't even speak the language."

Opening the door to our room, we saw right away that something was wrong. For a long second it looked like nobody was there at all. Geez, maybe they're out looking for us, I thought. But first we heard their voices and then we

51

discovered them—all of them. They were on their knees. The whole class was crawling around on the floor except for Molly, who was scrunched in front of the chalkboard. She ducked behind the teacher's desk when she saw us.

"Careful!" Miss Ivanovitch called out in a high, shaky voice. She was kneeling with a couple of kids over by the pencil sharpener. She rose and tiptoed toward us, searching the floor at each step. "Oh, *do* be careful where you walk."

I looked at the floor, too, expecting to see a shattered jar of yellow paint, a smear of white paste, or maybe even a tile missing with a vast hole opened up to the cafeteria below us. But nothing seemed to be strange about the floor at all.

"Jenny has lost a contact lens," Miss Ivanovitch explained. "It's one of the new kind that's made of something practically invisible like gelatin, and the poor dear is so upset."

Jenny did look upset. Arms folded on her desk, she was resting her head on them, and her shoulders were shaking. I never even knew she *wore* contact lenses.

"We're helping her search," Miss Ivanovitch went on, scanning the floor. "Unfortunately, she doesn't know where she was when it dropped out. It could be anywhere underfoot." She fingered the flowers on her blouse nervously, dropped to her knees again, and craned her neck under a desk, jangling her jewelry.

Jenny lifted her head and I could see by her grin that her shoulders had been shaking with laughs, not tears. At the chalkboard Molly picked up a piece of yellow chalk and wrote, "Boys I, Girls II."

Nick looked at Molly's scoreboard, lifted his eyebrows, and poked Marshall, who started planting his feet firmly as he marched back to his seat.

"Watch out, young man!" Miss Ivanovitch called, and everyone snaking around on the floor stopped to see what was happening. "Young man, that contact lens is very fragile. I said very clearly it was fragile." Marshall didn't pay any attention. "*'Fragile'* means if you step on it you'll *break* it!" she yelled, not very patiently.

Marshall turned around and looked sadly at her, but kept blasting up the aisle to his desk next to the bulletin board. He scraped the chair loudly as he sat.

Miss Ivanovitch blinked. She couldn't believe that dear boy was doing what she'd asked him *not* to, especially when she'd been careful to explain the hard word.

"Oh," Nick said, snapping his fingers like he'd just remembered something, "I bet you don't know about Marshall."

The kids on the floor quieted down and stared at Marshall, trying to figure what there was special to know about him. He bent toward his desk, tore a piece of square paper from his pad, and started folding.

"Marshall is Japanese," R.X. blurted out. Marshall turned his head away from Miss Ivanovitch and winked at Trevor on the floor next to him. Trevor collapsed on his back and started kicking his feet, he was laughing so hard. Miss Ivanovitch glanced quickly around at the rest of the class. Most of them were laughing, too. Then she stared at Marshall again. His face was turned away so all she could see was his San

Francisco T-shirt and springy black hair. It was true that even from the back Marshall didn't look Japanese. Miss Ivanovitch smiled slightly as though she might laugh, too.

"What R.X. means," Nick explained with a very straight face, trying to save us, "is that Marshall just moved to Stockton from Japan last month. He'd lived over there all his life and he doesn't speak any English yet. Only a word or two—maybe three. Before too long he'll start English lessons, but he likes it better now if you don't fuss. I tell you what, I'll look on the bottoms of his shoes to see if Jenny's lens stuck to either of them." He tiptoed toward Marshall's feet.

"What Marshall does," I went on with the story, "is he sits at his desk all day and folds origami because that reminds him of home. *Or-i-ga-mi!*" I called. Marshall nodded his understanding, smiled a small, sad smile, and held up this fancy purple kangaroo. A few of us clapped. Since there were also a few giggles, I went on, "We try to laugh a lot with him to cheer him up."

Miss Ivanovitch, trapped, clapped and laughed with us. It was actually a very impressive kangaroo. Marshall raised his eyes toward the ceiling and looked glum, like he was dying for Tokyo and some good old-fashioned raw squid.

"I've *got* it," Nick yelled, falling to his knees next to Marshall's desk. "I've found Jenny's lens."

Jenny, who had been peeking over her arms, raised her head. "You're kidding," she said. She picked her way slowly around the kids on the floor to the place where Nick was kneeling and narrowed her eyes at the piece of cracked plastic Nick held on the tip of his finger. Miss Ivanovitch peered, too.

While their heads were together, Molly was busy again at the chalkboard. The rest of the class kept fooling around on the floor, talking, taking books out of other kids' desks, and stacking them up in a row like standing dominoes.

When Nick, Jenny, and Miss Ivanovitch came out of their huddle, Jenny moaned, "That's nothing *like* my very fragile contact lens. I kn-kn-know I'll never find it. Ever. Ohhhhh," she blubbered, putting the back of her hand on her forehead.

I watched Molly drop low and crawl away from the chalkboard, inching down the middle aisle. In five minutes more it would be recess. So far we'd done no school work at all.

"Perhaps we should call your mommy," Miss Ivanovitch said, resting her arm on the sobbing shoulder. Jenny stopped moaning at once. "My *mommy*," she said flatly, "lives in Kankakee," which was true, even though it didn't sound like it. "My *daddy* is a psychiatrist in Chicago, and he'd put me on stale bread and water if I bothered him at the office."

Trevor and David, sitting on the floor near the windows, were lobbing wads of paper into the wastebasket and mostly missing. The fat paper balls kept colliding in midair, so the floor was littered with them. When David made two baskets in a row, he got up and bonged the Chinese gong still there from the Ting Tang Show.

Molly, meanwhile, had gotten all the way back to her desk. She and Marshall were the only ones sitting down. "Jenny might just have forgotten to put her contact lens in this morning," she called over the din.

Jenny smiled at Molly. "I *might*," she said, "at that. When I get home from school, I'll be sure to check."

Miss Ivanovitch looked from one girl to the other. Her shoulders drooped.

The gong sounded again. Rolf was taking his turn.

"Pfutzenreuter," she said, raising her voice, "you put that hammer down this instant! Everyone return to his or her own seat." Rolf rang the gong again, but gently. "The lens has been found. Or rather, it—"

Somebody tapped the first of the dominoed books and they slapped sharply to the floor. The racket of talking and laughing got louder and louder as kids headed more or less back to their places.

But Miss Ivanovitch stood completely still in the middle of the room, her hands clutching her skirt. She was looking, bewildered, at the chalkboard. Her eyes were wide with astonishment, but they weren't quite crying.

We stared, too. One by one, the kids stopped talking as they saw what she saw. It wasn't the scoreboard that got her, though now it said, "Girls III, Boys II." She couldn't know what that meant. It was her name. While everybody else was searching the floor for The Emperor's New Contact Lens, Molly was working on Miss Ivanovitch's name. She had added a couple of marks to SVETLANA, erased ANOV from the last name, and made a few other fast changes.

The announcement now read in big red block letters:

MY NAME IS SWEAT-LANA
I'VE GOT AN ITCH
I'M YOUR NURD

From the room next door we could hear a high, thin voice rise over the low mutter of the class. It was their sub shouting, "I was not, my friends, born yesterday." And then they, too, were quiet.

The bell rang. "Recess!" Marshall called into the silence. We grabbed kickballs from the bashed-up Styrofoam box where the school ones were kept and ran to our lockers.

"That's one of the three words he knows," Nick called back, loud enough for Miss Ivanovitch to hear. "Geez," he said to me, "can't he keep his mouth shut?"

I closed my eyes. This is *too* awful, I thought. Now she'll tell Miss Hutter and Miss Hutter will make us write our parents letters about it and then she'll tell Mr. Star and he'll start being grim instead of fun and then we'll be the ones to sink to the bottom of the deep blue sea.

6

HAVE A NICE DAY!!!

The snow was falling so fast we were afraid Miss Hutter might be there barring the outside door. If she was, we were going to argue. There was a lot to talk about and inside recess meant staying in the room. Staying in the room meant being overheard. Lockers slammed all around and kids were covering their mouths as they laughed, like they were telling dirty jokes. I could hear them saying "Sweat-land" and "Stink-llama" and then laughing some more.

Nick and I zipped our coats as we ran, but even then we just tied with Molly and Lisa getting to the door. Miss Hutter was there, all right, but all she said as she watched the four of us forge out into the blizzard was, "Remember, boys, no snow-balls," as though no girl ever threw a snowball in her whole life.

Outside, the wind was whirling so hard that in some places

you could see the blacktop and in others the drifts were way up over the tops of our hiking boots, almost to our knees.

"What I want to know is, how are you keeping score?" Nick asked Molly. "Not that it matters, since points don't count, but I'd say we're way ahead of you."

Molly started drawing lines in the snow with the toe of her boot. "I'm only counting *important* things like our switching names and the contact lens caper and my changing Sweatlana's message on the board." She chewed on her mitten a minute. "I gave you one for leaving the room and one for Marshall's Japanese, even though they *barely* counted."

"What about the crossing-guard story?" I asked.

"Excuse us," Lisa said, "but we've got, like, a lot to talk about," and she and Molly headed toward the jet slide. It's this big swept-wing slide that on warm days lots of kids can go down at once. In winter it makes a perfect shelter from the wind. Every single girl was huddled under it to talk about the sub.

The dry snow was not good for packing, but it would have been great to scoop it up by the armful and heave a batch under the jet slide. You couldn't miss, the girls were so neatly packaged in one space. But even things *like* snowballs were strictly forbidden. For throwing snow Miss Hutter sent you home. And if your mom worked, like mine does, she called her at work, and then your mom really let you have it when she got home. Then, even if it was sloppy joes for supper, they didn't taste good because your mom was mad. Miss Hutter stood there at a big cafeteria window spying on us, so we decided not to bother snowing the girls, but just to make plans of our own.

Nick herded the boys over to a corner near the spit pit. As we passed, I glanced over the rail and noticed that it didn't look half bad all piled up with clean snow. But everybody knew what was underneath, so the white icing didn't fool us for a minute. It was like a coat of paint over a bicycle held together by rust.

I looked over to see how Miss Ivanovitch was surviving. She'd put on a purple down coat and fuzzy black boots, but she had nothing over her ears to keep her from hearing us talk if the wind was right. Her back was tight against the brick wall, and her arms were crossed to keep in the warmth. While she didn't look ready to kick up her heels with happiness, there weren't any big, fat tears freezing on her cheeks, either. I wondered if she still loved little children.

"How do we know," Rolf asked, as we got into a football huddle, "how do we know who sinks her? I mean, what if it was right now that she started bawling?"

"I think," Nick said, thinking, "that it goes to the ones who did the last thing before she gives up. Right now," he sighed, "the girls would probably win."

"Yeah," I said, staring down into the pit, imagining things under the snow, things like frozen wads of Hubba Bubba, scrunched up test papers with C– written on them, and hibernating fungus. Then we all stared at Sweat-lana to see if she could take fourteen eyes looking at once. When she felt our whammy, she moved around the corner, closer to the jet slide. Maybe she thought she was safer near the girls. Maybe she'd decided it was us who'd changed her name to Sweatlana I've Got An Itch.

No matter how hard we tried, we couldn't think of anything that good ourselves. Marshall still needed to finish our fleet of planes, and Nick and I would buy a bag of rubber bands after school. But that was for tomorrow, and tomorrow might be too late. For a while we tried just kicking the ball, but, like our ideas, it kept sinking into the snow. Marshall and R.X. raced around making fresh tracks and tackling each other in the drifts. Still, nobody came up with anything else spectacular to do to the sub and it was only eleven o'clock, with almost the whole day left.

"Hey, how about watches?" Trevor asked suddenly. He was lying flat on the ground, flapping his arms and legs, making a snow angel. "Everybody wearing one?" Everybody wasn't. "Look, wear them tomorrow," he said, as we gathered over him and watched him finish his wide-winged angel.

We all had watches that were alike because of a sale at Dominick's, the big supermarket on Green Bay Road. Actually, it wasn't as much a sale as a special deal. Your family was supposed to save $300 worth of the pink cash register slips they gave out from October through December. The whole thing was to make you shop there, but if you did and saved the pink receipts, you could buy a digital watch

61

with an alarm for just $8.99. It was such a great deal that almost every boy in fourth grade got one for Christmas or Hanukkah. When you're in fourth grade you start feeling a little weird wearing the Star Wars watch your grandmother gave you when you were just learning to tell time, so you hide it in the junk under the bed or in the back of the drawer with the sea shells. Then you tell your folks you lost it at the swimming pool or something, but you don't throw it away because it will be good to take apart on a dull day. Anyway, most guys came back after winter vacation wearing a new Dominick's special with an extra hole poked in its black plastic band to make it small enough.

"If you don't have one, borrow one from somebody," Trevor said. "Then we all set them to go off at—I don't know—ten-thirteen tomorrow morning." He got up and shook himself clean. "What do you think? By then she ought to be pretty much worn down. Maybe that'll be the end of it."

Marshall, who was being very, very careful not to say a word, patted Trevor on the head like he thought old Trev was a terrific sub sinker. Actually, though, nobody expected a chorus of seven alarm beepers to make anyone get hysterical, but it did sound like fun. We could synchronize them like spies do on television.

That's all the plans we had.

"Time to go in," Miss Ivanovitch called, and we dashed to the door. I had the feeling if we didn't go in soon, the storm would bury us like old bubble gum. The girls came running from their shelter, hopping through drifts, scraping at snow with their mittens. Miss Ivanovitch stood at the door, waiting.

"Now I want you to tiptoe quietly up the stairs, children," she said. "Miss Hutter mentioned to me that you were a little bit too rowdy on the way out. I know you don't want to disturb the other boys and girls who are working. So let's all keep our lips locked." She turned an imaginary key in her mouth, took it out, and flung it toward the playground. Once her hand was free of the let's-pretend key, she reached to open the door. But before she'd budged it an inch, the girls let her have it. *Zap, paw, slam, socko,* five, six, seven, eight, nine snowballs smacked her from behind or got the door she was pulling at. Only nine. Some girl hadn't thrown one. Unfortunately, Miss Hutter was not at any window. If all the girls got sent home, they would have had to forfeit. But nobody was there to send them home. Nobody stood there but Miss I've Got An Itch.

Her lips still locked tight and the only key lying in a drift, she leaned over, scooped up a huge wad of snow, and, letting the ball warm in her bare hands, packed it tight. When it was just the way she wanted it, she tossed it straight up about a foot, caught it, and eyed us to make sure we were watching close. Then, without a word, she wound up and smashed that snowball flat on the nose of the jet slide. Giving us a little half smile, she turned around, opened the door, and went inside.

The kids in 4A, who'd been with their sub building a

snowman on the far side of the playground, were on their way in, too. They saw the shot and whistled. We didn't whistle because our jaws were hanging open.

Inside, we slowly hung our coats up in our lockers and stamped up the stairs to our room, our fingers and noses and toes still red and cold. As we thawed, we settled in for the next round. It began to occur to me that it wasn't just boys against girls anymore. The sub was in it, too.

The writing on the board was gone, both her name and our score. Even Mr. Star's math assignments left over from the day before had been erased. She must have decided to start out with a clean slate before she came down to recess. After she'd cleaned it, though, she'd drawn a picture with bright yellow chalk, a three-foot smiley face that had a grin from one circle eye to the other. Below the face, down near the chalk tray, she'd written, "Have A Nice Day!!!" Nobody smiled back at the face but her. We were not having a nice day and didn't want her telling us to.

Marching up to the front of the room, she sat on Mr. Star's desk again to start over, full of confidence, fresh from her bull's-eye. Her grin, though, like the one on the smiley face, was too wide, and she started off with a laugh that was too loud.

"Well," she said, chuckling, "I guess you've really put one or two over on me this morning." She swung her feet from side to side, and chewed on her bottom lip a minute before finally explaining, "I guess you got away with what you did because I did my student teaching with kindergartners and their regular teacher was there with me all the time, so I just didn't *know* about fourth graders. I mean, those five-year-olds were just so cute and cuddly. Oh, you're cute, too, of course, but you are also very, very funny. I guess," and the strange chuckle came again, "what I didn't realize is that fourth graders have such a terrific sense of humor." She beamed her appreciation of our humor.

It must have been hard smiling that wide at seventeen straight faces. Molly's was totally sour. She, for sure, didn't like Miss Ivanovitch fake laughing at things *she* thought were sure-fire sub sinkers. I noticed that Miss Ivanovitch wasn't going goochie-goo any longer. She was trying to talk to us now like we were buddies who had managed to pull a good practical joke on her. She smiled warmly.

Aretha smiled back. I wondered if she was the one who hadn't thrown a snowball.

"Well," Miss Ivanovitch said finally, "now that *you* know that I know, maybe we can just be friends. What do you say?"

There was a long silence and then Nick spoke up. "I say that we're five minutes late for music class and Mrs. Franchini won't like it one bit."

Miss Ivanovitch was getting smarter. Before believing him, she checked the schedule on Mr. Star's desk. It *did* say "Music" at 11:15 on Thursday, but that's all it said.

"Where do you *go* for Music?" she asked.

The girls already had a plan. Molly and Lisa stood up,

linked arms, and led the whole class the longest way possible to the Music Room. Aretha walked with Miss Ivanovitch, but I could see from the way the girls looked at her that she'd be afraid to tell. First, we tromped all the way to the other end of the school on the second floor, past the Resource Center and the third grades, stopping off at fountains on the way to get drinks, and then down the stairs by the sixth grade rooms, and all the way back the whole length of the school again.

R.X. and I stopped at the gym to watch the little kids play. They were using the parachute. The whole class was gathered around the edge of this humungous, real parachute. The gym teacher, Ms. Lucid, was calling out, "Lift!" The little kids raised it up, flapping their arms. The air gathered underneath so the parachute puffed out like a huge dome, then practically picked them up off their feet. When it had mushroomed out at its biggest, every second kid around the edge let go and ran like mad underneath, looking for a new place to hold on before the parachute collapsed on the floor. They were having a great time.

Then we strolled past the Art Room and the second grades before we got to the Music Room, which was just next to the cafeteria on the first floor. When we finally made it, our music teacher, Mrs. Franchini, said, "I'd about given up on you," and Molly told her with a sigh, "We got started late. We've got a substitute teacher today who's never even been in this school before." Heading back to her seat, she said, "She doesn't know much." Mrs. Franchini gave her a warning frown.

Out in the hall, Miss Ivanovitch heard Molly and flinched. I was standing next to her. "You don't have to go in with us," I told her. "Mr. Star never does. But you are supposed to come for us at noon."

She didn't believe me. And she walked right in behind the class like a Russian princess just back from a windy sleigh ride. She was still wearing her fuzzy black outside boots.

"You don't have to stay," Mrs. Franchini said kindly, "just come back in half an hour." She took Miss Ivanovitch's arm and leaned toward her. "Stop in at the teachers' lounge, room 115, and get a cup of coffee. You look as though you might need a rest."

Miss Ivanovitch smiled first at her and then at me. Right then I think she decided I was a truth teller and a friend. "Thank you, Hobie, my dear," she said.

As Miss Ivanovitch turned away, I heard Mrs. Franchini say, "Nicholas Rossi, it's time to start singing and stop talking. Or I'll make mostaccioli out of you, head to toes."

Nick grinned. Both of them have Italian names, and she's always teasing him like that.

"With Parmesan cheese," he told her, as if what he meant was, "Certainly, Mrs. Franchini."

"All right, then," she said, sitting down at the piano, and we started right off with two songs we were going to do for the Fourth Grade Sing in March. First, "I can Sing a Rainbow" and then one that is funnier than its name, "Be Kind to Your Parents." I knew my mom and dad would, for sure, like the part where it goes:

Remember they're grown-ups, a difficult stage of life.
They're apt to be nervous and over excited,
Confused from the daily storm and strife.
Just keep in mind, tho' it sounds odd, I know—
Most parents once were children long ago.
Incredible!

My mouth was wide open shouting "Incredible!" when I glanced out the door and saw Miss Ivanovitch standing there, not as hidden as she thought. She was listening. Maybe to the singing. Probably not, though, because we weren't all that good yet. I think she was listening to see how it was done. In Mrs. Franchini's class nobody was scraping chairs or crawling on the floor or scribbling on the chalkboard. I believe she wanted to learn how to make us into good little children.

Just as I was looking, she peeked around the corner, laughed when she saw me, and waved with both hands like she did when we left with the cafeteria count. I had the sinking feeling that I was fast on my way to being Hobie, my dear, the substitute-teacher's pet.

When the time came to leave she was still around the corner, waiting, and she led us, the short way, back up the fourth grade steps. Molly joined Nick and me, a smirk on her face. "She may talk big and know how to throw a handful of snow, but I think she's scared," she said, walking backward down the hall in front of us. "I hope you guys were over there spitting into the pit at recess to make it more gross because it's going to be all yours from now on. We've scored a whole lot more points than you have."

"Ha!" I answered. "Ha! Ha! That's what you think."

"Points don't even matter. It's the final flood that counts," Nick told her.

"You know," Molly said, "my grandmother told my mother about Mr. Star practically barfing in class, and my grandmother said she *anticipates* that we will all be sick by tomorrow. She said Mr. Star was all germy and that he had no business, no business at all, being in school yesterday."

"I've heard," I told her, "it's the Shanghai flu that's going around. I think your grandmother brought it back with her in that box of stuff. I think there are Shanghai flu germs all over her Chinese cricket cage. I think it's not empty at all. I think it's filled with billions of million-legged, bug-eyed germs. If you want to know what I think, I think that because you brought your grandmother's germy stuff to school, the flu is *your* fault."

Molly tossed her hair and raced up the stairs ahead of us. At the top she turned around and said, "I am rubber and you are glue. Whatever you say bounces off me and sticks to you," stuck out her tongue, and disappeared into the room.

"She is definitely not cueshee. She is oosick, a dwerp, and a squird. And we can't let her win," Nick said. He was right.

7

THE FANGED FACE

The sign on the principal's office read "IN." That didn't mean Miss Hutter was in. That meant *we* were. The sign had a picture on it of a fat gray cloud with a mean eye and O-shaped lips blowing out a mouthful of stormy weather. We were staying in because by lunchtime the snow had gotten so deep or the temperature so low or the wind so wild that she was afraid she'd lose a kid or two if she let us out. We were sorry. Out days are better. After we ate our hot dogs and Jell-O in the cafeteria we had to go into the auditorium to watch movies. Nick and Rolf and I sat together, but we didn't watch too close. One movie was on the life cycle of the monarch butterfly. The other one was about sharks. Nothing but leaves and little fishes got eaten up in either movie. I'd have given each one about half a star.

The auditorium was hot and most kids were dressed for

cold, so the whole place smelled like wet boots and damp hair. By the time the first bell rang, we were pretty much zonked out by the dark and the steam heat, but we slogged back upstairs anyway, ready to give sub sinking another try.

People had been talking about it all through lunch, thinking of things they wanted to do, remembering stuff their brothers and sisters and even parents had told them *they'd* done. So when we got to the room, everybody's plans started rolling right away. The line at the pencil sharpener had at least five girls in it. At one-eighteen all the boys dropped their math books flat on the floor. They made a giant smack and a few people jumped. Unfortunately, though, Miss Ivanovitch was in the hall at the time, trying to reel in the kids who were out there talking. The girls started raising their hands to go to the washroom just as Rolf let a handful of paperclips slip through the slits in the radiator under the window. For a good twenty minutes those clips rattled and pinged like hail on a metal roof.

The place was so up for grabs that Molly wasn't even adding anything to what *she'd* decided the score was. But, somehow, on the way to the pencil sharpener, she did manage to detour past the chalkboard slow enough to grab a piece of red chalk and draw on the huge smiley face a pair of mountain-shaped eyebrows that met in the middle like Miss Ivanovitch's. And on the way back from turning her pencil into shavings for the thirteenth time, she added two long red fangs to the smile.

Marshall wasn't making any noise. He sat at his work,

happy as a pigeon on a ledge, stuffing his desk with new paper airplanes and making an occasional bird. When Miss Ivanovitch passed his chair, he gave her a crane folded out of blue paper, which she stuck in her thick hair. It perched there like it was sitting in a black nest.

"Class," she announced, "I have found Mr. Star's lesson plans. They were right in the top drawer." She shuffled through the pages. "It's a little late to start the new unit in Social Studies, so we'll begin Local Government tomorrow." R.X., standing back by the sink, groaned. "Instead, we'll forge right on to Math. The assignment sheet says that you are to do pages 89 and 90 in your math workbooks." The girls at the pencil sharpener couldn't hear her so she had to repeat it. "I want those pages on Mr. Star's desk today so I can correct them before he gets back. I suggest you take out your workbooks and start on them right now." She waited, and when none of the talking stopped, added, "Or else."

"Or else what?" Rolf asked, and we all listened for the answer. My dad always says not to make threats you can't deliver on. For a second Miss Ivanovitch's face had the same panicked look our cat Fido gets when somebody turns on the vacuum cleaner. He doesn't know whether to run or attack. Finally, she shrugged and said, "Or else Mr. Star won't get them."

It wasn't easy to argue with that. But then, I thought, after all, we'd got out of both Language Arts and Science in the morning by just fooling around. Might as well go ahead and do the math. We'd have to sooner or later anyway.

"But Mr. Star hasn't taught us how to *do* any of this," R.X. complained. "We don't even know what these problems are all about. I think you must have got the page numbers wrong."

She looked over the assignment "You mean you're in fourth grade and don't know how to do simple multiplication? I don't believe it." She for sure had stopped thinking we didn't know 2 plus 2. Now she had us ready for algebra.

Staring over my shoulder, she saw that I'd already finished two problems. I should have covered them with my hand.

"Hobie is doing the work," she said in triumph, and R.X. looked daggers at me. "Perhaps when he's finished he can help you."

Miss Ivanovitch gave me an encouraging smile. But as she checked over my math, I noticed that her eyes kept wandering to my T-shirt. Maybe, I thought, she feels sorry for me. Maybe I ought to explain about the melted crayons in the dryer so she won't think my clothes are too weird.

Nick, workbook in hand to ask a stupid question, was standing next to us. He had noticed her looking at my shirt, too. "I can see you like Hobie's shirt, Miss Ivanovitch," he said. "Did you know that Hobie's mother is an artist?" I gagged a little because my mother is about as much an artist as Fido is. She's a physical therapist and helps people who are just getting over strokes and car accidents and things. She can hardly even draw smiley faces.

"Maybe you've heard of her," he went on. "Mrs. Hanson is her name. She makes these fantastic designer T-shirts and jeans like you see on TV, and Hobie here wears them almost every day to school as advertisements. She uses mostly red colors, you'll notice. That's her trademark."

Miss Ivanovitch wasn't going to let him put anything over on her. "Did your mother really do this?" she asked me, barely disguising the fact that she thought the shirt looked disgusting.

"Yes," I said, telling the truth, "she did it last October."

"It's not signed, though, is it, Hobie?" Nick asked, pulling back my shirt and peering in at the neck label.

"No," I said, "this one's not signed."

"He has some underwear in the same pattern."

"That's not signed, either," I told her.

"I expect you'd like Hobie's mother to make you one or two. They're pretty expensive, though. Close to a hundred dollars. Maybe you could pay in installments."

"Miss I-*van*-o-vitch!" Lisa called.

Rolf had moved over to the empty desk next to Lisa's and was chewing on the tail of his pink plastic ball-point fish, swinging his untied gym shoes back and forth. He kicked the bottom of Lisa's desk with each swing.

"Miss Ivanovitch!" Lisa called again, waving her hand in the air urgently.

"Yes, Molly."

Several girls giggled at how incredibly dumb you'd have to

be *still* not to know that Lisa wasn't Molly.

"Pfutzenreuter is kicking my desk."

"I am not." He banged her chair again for telling.

"You are, too!"

He stopped kicking. "I am not."

"You were!"

"Who says?"

"I say!"

"Well, who do you think *you* are, the princess and the pea?"

Using the soles of both her feet, she shoved his desk about a foot away.

"Children, you mustn't fight," Miss Ivanovitch warned. But she didn't say, "Or else."

Rolf started wiggling his fish pen toward Lisa like it might scribble zigzags on her neck.

"Dwerp! Squird! Racket!" Lisa yelled, swatting her workbook at him.

"Lisa!" Molly hissed. "Cut it out. It's a trap. He *started* it. It's his point."

I think he was just kicking, myself, but if she wanted to turn it into a point for us, that was all right with me.

Lisa clenched her jaws, gave Rolf a double evil eye, and bashed him on the head with her workbook.

"Lisa!" Molly warned.

Miss Ivanovitch suddenly did not look upset by the fight at all. Instead she stared steadily at Molly with just a flicker of a smile.

Molly glanced up at her and gulped, like she'd just swallowed a live fly.

Miss Ivanovitch said nothing at all, but just moved to the other side of the room to try to coax Marshall, who didn't speak English, into doing the part of the math that didn't need any. I leaned over to Molly and said, "I'm pretty sure she heard you when you called Lisa 'Lisa.' "

"You think so?" she whispered back. Then she shrugged her shoulders and smiled. "If she heard me, why didn't she *say* something about it? I would have." She wrote a quick note, which she passed back to Michelle, who raised her hand and asked Miss Ivanovitch if she would please help her with a story problem.

Miss Ivanovitch left wide-eyed Marshall and turned to her.

"Let's see now. This doesn't look at all hard. 'Four classes are going on a field trip to the Nature Center,'" Miss Ivanovitch read aloud. "'If there are twenty-eight children in one class and twenty-nine in the other three, how—'"

"*Shhhhhh!* Please! I'm trying to concentrate," Jenny complained. What she was really trying to do, it seemed to me, was multiply using a pencil that by now was only about an inch long.

While the sub had her back turned, explaining about the number of kids on the field trip, Molly was at the board again. "Girls ~~IIII~~ I," she wrote, "Boys IIII," though I couldn't, for the life of me, figure out where she got those numbers. She was just trying to scare us, but it didn't work on me.

Confucius says, "Phony numbers don't squeeze out real tears."

R.X. and Trevor got up, stretched, ambled over to the sink, and started to wash their hands. The math must have gotten them dirty.

When Miss Ivanovitch announced finally that it was gym time, she looked to the front of the room and saw the new score, as well as the red fanged and eyebrowed face. She didn't look anywhere close to tears about it, though. Instead, she walked straight up to the chalkboard, and, just when I guessed she was going to erase the whole thing, she picked up the yellow chalk and drew a pair of earrings with bells on the ends where the Face's ears would be. Then, after smiling back at Molly, she added to the scoreboard, "Sub II."

Those numbers I could figure. Her first was the snowball. What the second one was, Molly and I both knew.

8

YOURS TILL
NIAGARA FALLS

Miss Ivanovitch didn't get lost again. She herded us down the steps and through the hall the fastest way to the gym, plucking people out of doorways and scooting them away from the water fountains.

"I stopped and looked in the gym on the way to Music this morning," Nick told me, pushing his trot to a gallop. "The third graders were parachuting."

"I know," I said, matching his steps, "I saw them, too." That's why we were both in a hurry. There was a chance that Ms. Lucid had kept the parachute out for us to use, too. The little kids mostly just lifted it and ran under, but we got to play ballgames with the parachute, puffing it up huge, trying to flip the ball on top, off to the other kids' side. The parachute was the best, the very best gym thing.

But even before we got to the gym, we stopped jogging, all of us. Our ears twitched. Today wasn't going to be the best. It was going to be the worst.

"This sub brought us rotten luck," somebody behind us said.

Worse luck than stepping on a stinkfish. From the gym we heard music. Not just any music, but "A Hunting We Will Go." Folk dancing music. The pits. That meant we were going to have to skip across the gym and circle around this little square on the floor, "to catch a fox and put him in a box and then we'll let him go." Then, after that record, Ms. Lucid would put on another one that meant holding hands. Sooner or later you have to hold hands to folk dance. But then when you do, the girls always wrinkle up their noses and say your hands are too sweaty and wave their own Arrid-dry hands in the air, refusing to hold yours again. After that, you look and feel even dumber skipping around the gym *not* holding hands. It's a no win.

Thinking about wet hands, we slogged toward the gym, practically in reverse, our lips curled. Miss Ivanovitch, though, just about flew. If Miss Hutter had been around she would have yelled, "No running in the halls," and with our luck Miss Ivanovitch would have collapsed on the floor and cried. Then Miss Hutter would have been the winner and champion, which wouldn't have done her a whole lot of good

79

since she never goes down into the spit pit anyway. While most of the class was still down the hall making faces at the fifth graders in the Art Room, our sub was already leaping into the gym toward the music, the first one there.

She was dressed for folk dancing, of course. I mean, she looked like she should sit right down on her heels and kick out her legs with her arms crossed.

"Oh, my," she announced, as soon as she managed to tug us all into the gym, "we're an uneven number today—seventeen. I wonder," she asked Ms. Lucid, "if I could join the children? I do love dancing."

"Take those boots off," Ms. Lucid answered sharply. "No street shoes on the gym floor."

Taking that to mean, "You're welcome to dance with your boots off," Miss Ivanovitch sat down and tugged away. In her black-and-red-striped stocking feet she was just about our size.

First off, Ms. Lucid lined us up. Then she put the needle at the beginning of the record again and turned up the volume on the old record player. Somebody stomped on the floor, and the needle skipped like a stone on water, shrieking at each bounce. Ms. Lucid frowned, dug in her pocket, and took out a quarter. She put it on the tone arm of the record player, to make it heavier, and tried again. This time the song blasted out, and she waved us forward.

As we dragged our feet through catching the fox and putting him in a box, it made us mad to watch Sweat-lana I've

Got An Itch skipping along. Even if you actually *liked* folk dancing, you weren't supposed to show it. But raising her knees high and tilting her head like the people on the record jacket, she didn't even notice our shuffling. Her eyes shone with happiness as she hummed along. Her bracelets clicked, and her earrings swung to the beat.

The idea of dancing the Virginia reel seemed to please her even more. And who do you suppose she chose to be her partner? No contest. Good old trustworthy Hobie Dear. Everybody scrunched up their shoulders, bent over, and laughed behind their hands when she clapped and said, "I'll take Hobie." If I had been Molly I would have moaned, "Oosick, cootie shot," and refused to dance with her, holding my hands behind my back. I couldn't do that, but my face was red all the way under my hair, making my scalp prickle, and it was all I could do to keep from running away.

In the Virginia reel you meet in the middle between these two lines of people and swing somebody around by the elbow. There are two ways to swing. Either you barely touch the other person like they have chicken pox and you don't want to catch it or you whirl the other person around like you're trying to orbit them around the moon.

R.X. was the first one up and he did OK with the first three, treating them kind of germy, but when he got to Jenny, he tried the orbit trick. Swinging her totally hard, he lost his grip and let her go spinning like a top as she slid off his elbow. She careened through the couples and flew head first into an amazed Miss Ivanovitch, who doubled up and skidded off backward on her bottom across the waxed gym floor. The blue origami bird blew out of her hair and hid in a safe spot on the sidelines.

Jenny yowled.

Miss Ivanovitch, the breath knocked out of her by Jenny's head, sat on the floor heaving for air. She'd caught the fall partly with her elbow, which was skinned and already starting to get red.

Jenny, who was flattened, too, buried her head in her arms and sobbed. She didn't look skinned.

"No fair," Molly said under her breath to R.X. "Violence is no fair." She edged around in front of Miss Ivanovitch to see if she was crying. The two of them stared at each other. We all gathered round.

"Are you hurt?" I asked, watching the blood rise to the surface of her skinned elbow.

She sucked in a load of air. "I haven't had a skinned anything since I learned to ride a bike," she said, taking another breath. "Makes me feel young again."

Ms. Lucid helped her up and told her to go down to the nurse to get a bandage. Then she looked us all over in disgust before focusing on R.X. "R.X. Shea," she said, practically leveling him with her voice, "you sit by that wall as still as a stone and remember that you are not and never will be The Hulk. Nor should you wish to be. People are not meant for hurling. What's more—"

At the door, Miss Ivanovitch cleared her throat and said, "Oh, I'm sure he didn't mean—"

Ms. Lucid continued on as though our sub wasn't there, which didn't seem polite to me. "What's more, R.X., tomorrow we're going to parachute and you are going to sit that one out, too. As will any of the rest of you," and she scanned the class, "who feel like pulling cute little tricks." She stalked toward the record player. "If you want to parachute tomorrow, then be on your best behavior today."

Listening to the threats of a real teacher, Miss Ivanovitch's eyes got big, and I wondered if she was picturing us—all but poor R.X.—jumping off the roof of the school into thick drifts of snow, little white parachutes over our heads. No matter what she thought parachuting was, I guess she was sorry she couldn't promise it to us to make us behave. Subs don't have anything to promise. They're not going to be around long enough to deliver. She picked up her boots and started, stocking-footed, down the hall.

Maybe she just wished, as she walked toward the nurse's office with a bleeding elbow, that she'd stuck to kindergarten with its cute kids with big eyes who sat on her lap and sucked their thumbs. I guess she hadn't come across those little kids who scream for their mothers and bite and wet their pants like Toby, Nick's little brother. He's only four, but his mother's afraid he's going to flunk nursery school. Twenty-five Tobys in one room. I couldn't even think about it.

We do-si-doed and bowed our way through the rest of the period until a smiling and still shoeless Miss Ivanovitch appeared at the gym door to pick us up and take us home.

"I'm sorry if I hurt you," R.X. said, running up to her in the hall. Nobody had even told him to say it. She murmured something to him I couldn't hear. Before long he dropped back to walk with me and whispered, "I did something I wish I hadn't."

"You didn't hit the sub with Jenny on *purpose* did you?" I asked him. I couldn't imagine his aim was that good.

"No," he said, "that's not it. I think Jenny's hands were all sweaty, or, you know . . ."

"You weren't even holding her hands," I told him, "you were swinging her by the elbow."

"Well, whatever it was, I was just turning her high speed. I didn't know she was going to be so *slippery*. What I did, though, that I'm sorry about, isn't *that*. I mean, I'm sorry about *that,* too, but . . ." He turned around to make sure nobody was listening. ". . . Before we left, Trevor and I were back in the corner fooling around at the sink, you know. And maybe nothing has happened at all, but before we left I stuffed a paper towel in the drain and turned the water on." He looked scared. "It's been on all through Gym."

"You're kidding."

"I'm not either. I thought it would be funny to come back to Niagara Falls. Now I'm afraid to go back. I thought maybe she'd see it and cry, and we could stop this dumb game. I hate it."

"Me, too," I told him, glad somebody else had said it first.

"Trevor had found these two balloons in his pocket," R.X. explained, "and during Math we went back to the sink to make water balloons out of them."

As we walked, I could imagine the waves washing across the floor of our room, down the steps in a water-fall, and out the door to the playground.

"So after we'd filled these two fat water balloons, I just decided, I don't know, just to let the faucet run." He grabbed the sleeve of my red-splotched T-shirt. "What can I *do*?" He stopped, scared, and started to turn back. "If I go straight to the office and say I have the flu, they'll believe me. Everybody else has it." He put his hand to his forehead to see if maybe he had a fever.

"That's a dumb idea," I said, pulling him along. "It won't stop the water."

"Yeah, but, listen, I practically break her arm in Gym, and now what if she finds out I'm—"

"Somebody's got to stop it," I said, starting to run, picturing Miss Ivanovitch opening the classroom door and being swept away in high tide.

We took the steps by twos, but Miss Ivanovitch had made it there before us.

Rushing into the room, we saw her fling herself at the faucet to stop the flow. Just as she turned off the water, one of the balloons floated lazily over the edge of the sink and burst *splat* in the lake that used to be our floor.

"I should have made boats instead of planes," Marshall said, shaking his head and leaning against the bulletin board for support.

She turned. "Your English is improving remarkably," she told him. "Tell me, how do you say, 'Where are the paper towels' in Japanese?" He just stared at her, not sure how to answer.

She took a deep breath and eyed us all. "This is too much, you know. This is *really* too much. You are . . . awful . . . undisciplined . . . downright vicious brats. And *you*," she said, looking straight at me, "you came running in here like you knew it was happening. I just can't *believe* it." There was maybe a half inch of water underfoot. She sloshed through it to the desk and picked up Mr. Star's seating chart.

"I am on my way to the office," she said, waving it in the air, "and I am going to explain to Miss Hutter, who must certainly know without my telling her, that you are impossible children. You are absolutely out of control." She banged her fist on the desk so hard you could tell it hurt.

"Oh, no, we're not," Molly said from where the girls had gathered away from the deep part, "we're not out of control at all. You are."

Nobody said things like that to a teacher and got away with it. Ever. The room was quiet except for the sound of water squishing.

I wanted to say something like, "Don't be mad at us, please." Or, maybe even, "I'm sorry." But I didn't.

Molly kept looking at Miss Ivanovitch's eyes. I hoped she wasn't going to cry, but it looked possible.

"If you go to the office and tell them you can't control us," Molly went on, "they won't let you come back here to sub again." Suddenly I felt like *I* was going to cry.

"I don't know that I want to come back," Miss Ivanovitch told her, her voice getting steadier. "Maybe I'll go someplace else where the boys and girls are nicer."

"Kids are kids," Molly said, shrugging. She waded over to the pencil sharpener for the fifty-third time.

We listened to the steady grinding as we watched Miss Ivanovitch move slowly to the door. Her soggy red-and-black stockings would leave wet footprints all the way down to the office. "And I don't want to hear another peep out of you," she said, slamming the door behind her.

There was a long silence and then a few kids started doing the old "peep-peep-peep" like baby chicks routine, but it wasn't funny this time.

Marshall opened the supply cabinet door and took out handfuls of the paper towels Miss Ivanovitch had asked him about, and tossed them to people around the room.

"Try sweeping some of the water into the wastebasket with them," he said. "We can squeeze the towels out into the sink. It's not stopped up anymore."

Nick got down on the floor with his bundle, but they soaked through so fast it looked hopeless, so he stood up again. "What idiot was it who did this dumb, stupid thing, anyway?" he asked, looking at Molly and Lisa, like he knew who.

"Not me," Molly answered, sweet as jelly beans. "None of *us* did it." All the girls shook their heads. "We're not vandals," Molly told him, though I bet she wished she'd thought of it herself. "This is the work of some sick juvenile delinquent."

"I did it," R.X. said, his voice low, but loud enough so that everybody heard. He stared down at the water shimmering at the base of the sink. "Before Gym I turned it on low. I mean, everybody was doing *something*. Somehow I didn't think about its being so . . . wet. I just thought it would be . . . funny, kind of." He sat down heavily at the nearest desk.

Some of the girls looked prim. The others looked scared. They will tell, I thought, as soon as Miss Hutter gets here. Some things are bigger than the silent treatment.

"We said *sink* her, R.X., not *drown* her!" Nick gathered a great wet wad of towels, weighed it in his hand for a minute, and then, like he wanted to wipe out the whole stupid mess, flung it hard at the ceiling.

It stuck like glue.

9

FAIR'S FAIR

When the door swung open Marshall was wringing out paper towels at the sink, watching them fall apart in his hands. Michelle had made a cardboard scoop and was pushing water toward a little plastic bucket. Lisa was standing on her chair. Half of the class was on the floor, trying, without much luck, to sop up water. The other half shifted their feet, not knowing what to do. The second we heard the doorknob turn, those of us on the floor had scrunched down as far as we could. The ones standing up had pushed back against the wall. Some people closed their eyes so they would be invisible. There was very little breathing.

When the door swung open, we thought it would be the end of the world. Instead, it was Miss Ivanovitch, three mops tucked under her arms, two buckets in her hands.

"Listen," she said, matter of fact, "I decided that my telling on you isn't going to clean up this deluge." Holding out the mops, she went on, "I borrowed these from the custodian. I told him we'd had a little flood but that we didn't need his help. I didn't think it fair to ask him to do it. Neither did he."

R.X. reached for one at once, but Miss Ivanovitch turned first to Molly.

"Here's one for you, Molly," she said, looking straight at her. I guess she must have thought it was Molly's flood, which wasn't fair, of course, because it wasn't.

Molly shook her head and motioned to Lisa up on the chair. "*That's* Molly," she said. "You must have forgotten."

Lisa's lip quivered. "But, I'm, like . . ." she whispered, ". . . not . . ."

Miss Ivanovitch and Lisa both searched the class, waiting to see if somebody would tell, but Molly stood up so straight and looked so sure of herself that nobody did.

Giving Molly one last pleading look, Lisa jumped down from the chair and took the mop in two fingers like it might, at any time, turn into a hissing rattlesnake. She stood there with it, pouting.

"Move!" Miss Ivanovitch ordered. And Lisa moved.

I didn't feel sorry for her, either. She's the one who wanted to change names and make people promise not to tell.

"*Please,* let me," R.X. called, grabbing a mop and attacking the water under the sink like he planned to soak it up in two seconds. He looked guilty as anything, but I guess he couldn't force himself to say it.

Aretha reached for the last mop and that made me *sure* she was the girl who hadn't thrown a snowball.

"The rest of you move the desks back from the deepest part near the sink to high land near my desk," Miss Ivanovitch told us. The room *was* on a slant. We'd never noticed it before. "Hobie, you and Nick man the wringers." Nick took one bucket and I took the other and every time a mop got full we stuck it in the wringer attached to the top of the bucket and turned the crank. Then we got somebody else to empty the water in the sink.

"Did you ever hear about the Sorcerer's Apprentice?" Miss Ivanovitch asked us, but nobody was sure they had. "I'll tell you about him tomorrow—if there *is* a tomorrow," she said, not sounding sure there would be. "Of course, he had magic to help clean up his flood, and all you've got is elbow grease."

Molly was back by the chalkboard fooling around again. Her score now read "Girls ⅲ II, Boys ⅲ I, Sub III." Nobody was paying much attention, though. Nobody was playing that particular game but her.

Miss Ivanovitch had taken over with one of the mops and when her back was turned, Trevor took a running start and skidded six feet across the slick floor, crashing into the radiator, and falling flat on his bottom.

"Here," she said, handing him the mop. "It's time you put all that energy into doing something useful."

With all the desks pushed to the front of the class where the water had barely reached, it looked like we were getting the floor ready for folk dancing or a wrestling match. At least it didn't, any more, look like we were clearing the lanes for a swim meet. Some of the classrooms have rugs. It's a good thing ours doesn't. If we'd hung it out the window to dry, it would have frozen to the brick. But it wouldn't have turned white overnight. The snow had stopped falling and we could see big patches of blue sky.

Kids whose notebooks were wet stood around by the radiator arranging them open so the pages would dry. Trevor, Lisa, and Miss Ivanovitch were still mopping. Rolf and Marshall were wringing. Some kids were sitting on top of desks, watching. And that's the way we were when the door banged open and Molly's grandmother came storming in, carrying a grocery bag over her raccoon-draped arm. This time she was wearing a hat that matched her coat.

"Hello, hello!" she boomed. "Or, as they say in China, 'Ni hao, ni hao!'" Her eyes searched the room for a teacher, a tall person in charge. When she spotted Miss Ivanovitch, mopping away in her striped stocking feet, like Cinderella on a bad day, she asked, almost speechless, "Pardon me, are you—"

"I am," our sub said, "Miss Ivanovitch. We have had a mishap, which we are correcting." She shifted the mop to her left hand and held out her right.

Mrs. Bosco shifted the grocery bag to her left arm, and they shook hands.

"I," she said grandly, "am Lucinda Bosco, Molly's grandmother," and she gestured to the front of the room where Molly stood just behind Mr. Star's desk. "The snowplows have cleared the streets, and it's a winter wonderland out there. I've brought a little treat in for the class. Fortune cookies and Hawaiian Punch. Being here yesterday was *such* a treat for me."

Miss Ivanovitch looked blank. She didn't know about yesterday. A sub is just today.

"Molly," Mrs. Bosco boomed, going over the teacher's head, "come here and get the treats!" Then she addressed us all. "I would have brought some hot Chinese tea, but I don't expect any of you drink it."

Drawing herself up as tall as she could, Miss Ivanovitch said, "You must be mistaken, *this* is Molly." She put her hand on Lisa's shoulder and guided her firmly over to Mrs. Bosco.

"*You're* the one who's mistaken, lady," Mrs. Bosco shouted. "What makes you think I don't know my own granddaughter? I've known her for ten years, and this child isn't my little dumpling." But she gave the bag to Lisa anyway. Hawaiian Punch is heavy.

"Class," Miss Ivanovitch said, not giving up that easy, "what is this girl's name?" She had not let go of Lisa's shoulder.

We didn't know what to do. If we said, "Lisa," that would be telling, and Molly made us all promise not to tell. If we said, "Molly," Mrs. Bosco would think we were all bananas.

I didn't mind sounding bananas. "Molly," I said. "Molly," Nick said. "Molly," Aretha said, grinning. "Molly," Lisa said, and she started giggling like crazy.

Mrs. Bosco pulled her hat down tightly on her head to make that, at least, secure. "Well," she said, "I don't know what's going on here, but I don't like it." Turning on her heel, she stormed out of the room and slammed the door behind her.

Lisa was doubled over with giggles. "You want to use the mop, Lisa?" she asked, holding it out to Molly. Everybody was laughing by now. We knew Mrs. Bosco might be headed down to tell Miss Hutter, but we still couldn't stop. Everybody laughed but Molly, who stood in front of the room with her teeth clenched in anger. Even Miss Ivanovitch was smiling. If Molly was still keeping points, Sub would have one added to it.

Mrs. Bosco swung open the door again and addressed us. "I don't see what's funny. I don't see what's funny at all. This looks like a disaster to me, a disaster pure and simple. I can't imagine what's happening in this room. Yesterday was so beautiful. Yesterday," she told Miss Ivanovitch sternly, "was an educational experience. I heard a beautiful, well-ordered report on China in this classroom. It was absolutely comprehensive, with excellent visual aids. The children told about Confucius's beautiful, beautiful philosophy, 'Do Not Do To Others What You Would Not Have Them Do To You.'"

Miss Ivanovitch blinked at us in wonder. " 'Do not do to others'?" she asked, shaking her head and starting to laugh. "*These* children?"

"They are marvelous boys and girls," Molly's grandmother

went on, shocked again about the sub. "I don't know what they have done to deserve such a . . . curious . . . substitute teacher." She looked around the room. "Molly, don't let them open the cookies." She harumphed and left. When she slammed the door, the room shook.

Miss Ivanovitch couldn't keep it in any longer. She grinned around at us standing there, our jaws hanging open. Shaking her head, she started to smile even wider, and finally she just threw back her head and began to laugh. But her huge, hiccupy giggle was stopped halfway out. From the ceiling there came a fat, slogging *splatch!*

Knocked free by the slamming door, the soggy wad of paper towels that Nick had flung up when he was mad came splashing down on Miss Ivanovitch's head. It sat there wetly, half on her black hair and half on her forehead, like a wrinkled trick hat leaking streams of water down her face and neck.

And that *was* more than she could take. She lifted off the hat, tipped it to us with a bow, and then lobbed it, *swish* into the water-filled wastebasket. She laughed and laughed, and we laughed with her. She laughed so hard that tears came to her eyes.

"Anybody got a Kleenex?" she asked between laughs.

There was a gasp or two and then suddenly a strange silence.

"Kleenex?" Molly yelped, like Miss Ivanovitch had asked us for a fistful of lighted firecrackers. "A Kleenex? I don't believe it," she whispered. "The sub is *crying*."

"A paper towel will do," Miss Ivanovitch said, grabbing one from a free pile and wiping her eyes and her runny nose.

"No fair!" Molly yelled. "She's laughing, that's why she's crying. That's no fair."

Giggling, Miss Ivanovitch asked her, "Am I not allowed to laugh, Lisa?"

"My name is Molly."

"Oh?" Miss Ivanovitch smiled. "Then I must have been mistaken after all. That *was* your grandmother?"

"You know perfectly well that was my grandmother. You're just out to get me." She stuck out her bottom lip and looked around the room. "All of you."

"Confucius says," Miss Ivanovitch said lightly, turning away, "that each person should grab a desk and put it back in its place. It's ten minutes to three. The place is still like a marsh, but I think it will probably dry out overnight." Spotting Nick and me, she said, "Do the crossing guards have to go now?"

"Oh, we're not really crossing guards," Nick told her. "You have to be in fifth grade to be a crossing guard. We're still too little."

"Too little? I'd long since stopped considering you little." She looked us over. "Good grief, I've learned a lot today. But I'm afraid I haven't taught you anything at all." She sighed. "Oh, Marshall, could you do me a favor?"

Marshall, who was helping scoot the desks back in place,

answered her in a strange language that wasn't English and sure wasn't Japanese. "Herro may watchie san chop suey oosick," he said with a straight face.

"Glad to hear it, because what I want to do now is see if those airplanes you have been slaving away on fly as good as they look. Do you have enough for everybody to have one?"

"Sure," he said. "Girls, too?"

"Girls are usually included in the pronoun 'everybody.' As am I."

"Then there's enough for everybody to have at least three," he said, and started passing them out.

I leaned over to Nick. "Well, did we sink her or not?"

"Sure," he whispered. "Fair's fair."

"*They* won't say it's fair."

"Maybe." He shrugged. "But we got real tears. You can still see the rivers on her face. The spit pit belongs to the girls for the rest of the year. We won fair and square."

We all gathered at the far end of the room near the chalkboard and Mr. Star's desk so we could make our planes fly the longest distance. Marshall threw the first one, and it whipped up to the ceiling and then took a dive, cracking up at once. He started explaining to us what had been the matter, something technical about balance, but nobody was listening. We were filling the air with paper, zooming planes up to the lights, skimming them just over desk level, looping them in tailspinning stunts. It was beautiful, as Mrs. Bosco would have said, beautiful.

But it was Miss Hutter who opened the door. She opened it so quietly that nobody even noticed. And when she and Mrs. Bosco breezed in, two planes flew out, still rising high down the hall. Aretha, who was taking such care in aiming that she didn't see Miss Hutter come in, threw her last plane as the principal stood there, gaping, in the doorway. Aretha's paper airplane sailed lightly, perfectly, gently down the length of the room. It was one of Marshall's best. Mrs. Bosco stepped briskly forward and caught it, like a large grandmother raccoon snapping a fish out of its stream.

They both stared at Miss Ivanovitch and her tear-streaked face.

The planes had all stopped, but one of the mops dropped out of its bucket with a crash.

Miss Ivanovitch cleared her throat. "It's . . . science," she explained in a slightly shaky voice. "We're having Science last period today. Our lesson is . . . aerodynamics. Earlier, for Social Studies, we found out rather a lot about the philosophy of Confucius, a beautiful philosophy the class had started to consider yesterday."

We did not move, but just stood there quietly waiting for the explosion that was bound to come.

"Miss Ivanovitch, I think we should speak for a moment alone in the hall," Miss Hutter said, her face grim. We were going to lose our sub, our sub who threw snowballs and paper planes, knew how to folk dance, and didn't rat on us when she should have. We were going to lose her for sure.

"The fourth grade has changed a great deal since I was in school," Miss Ivanovitch went on, not moving an inch toward the hall. She threw her head back and her earrings jingled merrily, but she looked nervous.

"Yes," Miss Hutter said, adjusting her glasses, "I suppose it has." Mrs. Bosco poked her with her elbow. "Oh, yes," she went on, "Mrs. Bosco has asked me to question you because she felt there was some mix-up about her granddaughter."

"That was *all* my fault," Miss Ivanovitch said, nodding seriously to Molly. "A simple case of mistaken identity. Right, Molly?"

Molly narrowed her eyes and looked as though she'd like to stick her tongue out as an answer. "Right," she said, sharply.

Lisa covered her mouth and giggled.

"Oh, by the way," Miss Ivanovitch asked, "how is Mr. Star? We've all been wondering."

"Yes, yes," we all said, eager to change the subject. "Yes, how?" we wondered loudly. "Has he stopped vomiting?" Nick asked, louder than he meant to.

"I earnestly, earnestly hope he will be back by tomorrow," Mrs. Bosco said, pushing the grocery bag into the corner away from our strange paper-plane-covered classroom.

Miss Hutter opened her mouth to answer, but her eyes had wandered back to the chalkboard and focused on the big smiley face there that still beamed its fanged grin.

"Tell me, Miss Ivanovitch . . ." she started, and then

paused, looking the rest of the question over her glasses.

"It's *art!*" Aretha called, the first to find her voice. "Miss Ivanovitch was just showing us how many, many ways you can change a smiley face into something else. It's amazing!" She dashed to the board and drew another circle next to the lady vampire. In it she put two dots for eyes, two eyebrows that slanted in, a grin, a little pointed beard, and half a curvy moustache.

It was me as half a Confucius.

This time Mrs. Bosco started to chuckle. She must have recognized the makeup from yesterday. "I meant to tell you," she said, thunking me on the back, "I meant to tell you yesterday that I have a Confucius-says joke from the time when I was a child. We told a lot of those in my day. Those were my favorite jokes." The raccoons of her coat shook like they meant to leap off and run away. "It's because of Confucius that I brought the treat today," she said, lifting fortune cookies and cans of punch out of the bag.

"I suppose I really shouldn't tell this." She giggled. "It's a trifle unseemly. But then I don't see why one shouldn't laugh in school, do you?"

Miss Hutter nodded politely and glanced at the clock.

"Do you know what Confucius says he-who-stick-face-in-punch-bowl gets?"

Nobody answered. We all laughed a little nervously, kind of embarrassed for her. "Oh, *Grandmother*," Molly groaned.

"Confucius says," she barreled on, anyway, "he-who-stick-face-in-punch-bowl . . . gets punch in nose." And she laughed until the tears rolled. "I learned that when I was in fourth grade."

"That's charming," Miss Hutter said as the bell rang. It was time to go home.

"Really, how *is* Mr. Star?" Miss Ivanovitch asked quickly. None of us moved to leave.

"Oh, oh, yes, I meant to say," Miss Hutter explained, "he's feeling much, much better. No temperature, calm stomach. Much better. He called earlier to say he expects to be back in school tomorrow."

Miss Ivanovitch's face fell. She looked disappointed. I couldn't believe it. She actually looked sorry not to be coming back for another day of us.

"But," Miss Hutter went on, "I told Mr. Star I wouldn't hear of it. You simply can't get rid of stomach flu *that* quickly. Tomorrow is, after all, Friday, and if he rests tomorrow and through the weekend, too, he should be in tip-top shape by Monday. So, I told him to stay home. And I planned to ask you, Miss Ivanovitch, whether . . ." She looked around the room. The windows were covered with steam from all the dampness, paper littered the floor. ". . . Under the circumstances, do you think you . . ." She wondered, I could tell, if she should go on, even if the sub pool was almost empty.

It was getting late. As kids rushed out to catch their buses, Mrs. Bosco handed each one a fortune cookie.

"Very funny," R.X. said, reading the little white strip of

paper that had been inside his. "This cookie tells me that through storm and strife, good sense rules my life."

"Before I came this morning, a friend gave me a big bag of caramels to bring to school," Miss Ivanovitch told Miss Hutter. "She said if I kept handing them out all day, the boys and girls wouldn't talk so much because their little jaws would be endlessly stuck together." She cradled her skinned elbow in her hand. "I laughed at that." She smiled at the kids who were leaving, and waved at Marshall with both hands. "All day, I thought about caramels, huge sticky taffy ones that might even glue children to their chairs. But tomorrow," she grinned at Miss Hutter, "I think I will do much better, even without candy."

Miss Hutter smiled back, took a deep breath, and hurried off to the office. "We'll see you tomorrow then," she called over her shoulder.

Molly raised her right eyebrow.

"I've decided to leave the Hawaiian Punch for tomorrow," her grandmother told Miss Ivanovitch.

"Will it go with tacos?" Nick asked. He folded a piece of paper and bit the crease to make it tight.

"By my count, the total number of really good ways to sink a sub," Molly said low to Nick, "was thirteen, and the girls had seven of them. How many more do you suppose there are?"

A filled blue water balloon quivered on the sink. In my pocket from early in the day there was a note to myself that said "Bring rubber bands!"

Molly took a fortune cookie from the bag and turned it over in her hand. "I don't feel like eating this," she said.

"I wouldn't, if I were you," Nick told her. "I already got the good one. It was, 'Your pound of pluck is worth a ton of luck.' Besides, yours probably says 'I see a spit pit in your future.'"

Molly's face turned green, like Mr. Star's had the day before. "Grandmother," she said, tugging at her arm, "we had better go home. I feel awful." And they rushed out the door, Molly's hair swishing.

"Well, she's sure not going to be here tomorrow," Nick said. "I would say she is definitely oosick."

"Yeah, and with her gone, I don't know," Jenny told Michelle on their way out. "She's the one with all the good ideas."

Miss Ivanovitch smiled.

Nick tucked the taco into his desk and winked at me.

Miss Ivanovitch's earrings jingled as she picked up a soggy airplane from the floor. She looked pleased. "So, Molly won't be here." She sighed in relief. Then her eyes lifted once more to the brown spot on the ceiling and she turned to us, her eyes open wide.

"You don't suppose, do you," she asked, "that they send in substitute kids?"